The Four Leaf

A Holinight Novella

Lee Jacquot

The Four Leaf

LEE JACQUOT

This is a work of fiction. Names, characters, businesses, places, and incidents, as well as resemblance to actual persons, living or dead, is purely coincidental.

Cover Design: Ria O'Donnell at Graphic Escapist

Editing & Proofreading: Mackenzie at NiceGirlNaughtyEdits

A Quick Note From the Author

The Four Leaf is a standalone novella in the Holinights series. None of these books need to be read in order.

It is a sweet, steamy, and fun read intended for mature audiences of legal adulthood age as it includes explicit consensual sexual scenes. It should NOT be used as a guide for kinks or a BDSM relationship.

The author is not liable for any attachments formed to the MCs nor the sudden desire to have someone chase you in the woods.

Reader discretion is advised.

For the readers who just want to smile after their book buddy gave them a rec that tore their heart out.

This one's for you.

Samantha

CHAPTER ONE

The desire to get shitfaced drunk and dance naked in my living room to songs from the nineties is strong right now. So strong, in fact, I have to make a mental list of pros and cons to keep from saying screw it and actually doing it.

But alas, the cons side is much longer, and the current scowl on my sister's face from across the bar is borderline murderous. Her perfectly arched brows are raised so high they nearly touch her hairline. And with the terrifying way her iconic plump lips are stretched into a tight line, I add another bullet point to my imaginary list.

They say twins can almost read each other's minds, but I don't think the gift is exclusive to womb buddies. My sister has always had this sort of radar when it comes to my bullshit, and the majority of the time she's able to stop my shenanigans *before* I even get the chance to commit to them.

So now, with her reading the internal struggle on my face, I already know I won't be vibing on my new washable rug while sipping wine and swaying to *Waterfalls* by TLC.

I sigh, both at my own resignation and my sister's triumphant smirk, before glancing back down at my clipboard– the reason I'm overwhelmed in the first place.

Chapter 1

Being the manager of a ritzy hotel on a main street is one thing that already comes with an array of never-ending duties. But add the fact that it's Saint Patrick's Day, and the city's parade marches right in front of the hotel, then, well, you have yourself a place with no vacancies and not an empty seat in the in-house pub.

The number of needy guests this year seems to be at an all-time high, while the amount of sudden renovation projects required is astronomical. Not only that, but the handymen in the area are either off, charging double, or booked up.

Go figure my parents' pride and joy would choose the busiest time of year to start giving me gray ends at the prime age of twenty-five.

It sounds like I'm complaining, and while yeah, I partially am, I do love this place and all the stress that comes with it. Even though it means I don't get home until after my weekly shows have aired and my cat has curled up in my spot, forcing me to maneuver around her. I mean, what kind of cat-mom would I be to disturb her when she's gotten comfortable? I'm the late one, after all.

With another pass over my list, I finally decide what to tackle first. I've become relatively handy with the old plumbing and figure with all the local festivities happening tonight, no one should be without a working faucet or stuck with a clunky-sounding toilet.

Glancing up to tell my sister I'll see her later, the large flat screen on the wall behind her catches my eye. Like ninety percent of the time, a sports channel plays across the screen. It's a recap of yesterday's rugby game with two USA teams, and one player is currently being showcased for his incredible performance.

Number twenty-four. Adrian Santiago Stokes.

My heart leaps into my throat when his hazel eyes and a

thick forest of black hair appear on the TV. To the rest of the world, he's exactly what they describe. Six-three, two hundred and fifty pounds of pure muscle, always contributing to seventy percent of the team's points.

But I know the man off the field. The man who tempts my heart with going into cardiac arrest. The one I've secretly wanted since the first butterfly took flight.

I sound like a total creep, but we actually grew up together. Our parents were longtime friends and when Adrian and I were around five, they all decided to renovate and open a relatively small historic hotel downtown.

As one can imagine, we spent countless hours together running down the halls before it officially became The Four Leaf. We played hide and seek in the areas that weren't off-limits or under construction. Did our homework in the massive kitchen, which was the only place with decent light. Got in trouble when we had sword fights with paint sticks, and always seemed to be sent to Boston Common Park to play until the sun finally set.

My sister, Adrian, and I grew up within these walls. Learned how to cook, fix a leaky pipe, and clean those small vents in the bathroom. My sister, Willow, figured out how to drive, thanks to the expansive parking lot. And Adrian taught himself how to play piano from the grand piano in the ballroom by just watching videos on YouTube.

Somewhere between all that, and a crap ton of other memories embedded around this place, I fell for him. I mean, how could I not? He was everywhere, in everything.

Whether he was helping me with math, or we were watching the newest release on Netflix, he tattooed himself into all of my best and worst moments, all the while stealing more of my heart. It was a crush that gripped me by the throat and didn't let go.

3

Until it did.

Kind of.

Naturally, I was always too scared to ruin my friendship with him, and after a small incident that gave me a very 'friend-like' nickname, I've had to learn to keep my feelings in check. But no matter what I tell myself about our completely platonic friendship, my body doesn't agree. The visceral response when I see him is slightly embarrassing, and don't get me started on the aftermath left in my panties.

But who can blame me? The man is one of those guys they made in stone back in Greece to depict the Gods, while also having the personality of your favorite German Shepherd. I know, comparing him to both a God and a dog, but it fits. The guy is loyal, kind, smart, strong, protective, and sexy as hell, while also slightly terrifying.

"Are you going to ogle Adrian all night, or actually start on that list?" My sister pops the top off a green bottle and hands it to an eagerly waiting patron. Her blonde ponytail whips back and forth as she moves gracefully behind the bar, performing some type of choreography only she and her barbacks know the footwork to.

I roll my eyes and tap my pen on the metal piece of my clipboard. "I was just thinking how convenient it would be if he were here."

It's not a complete lie. Adrian did more work than my sister and I combined when we were growing up here. Probably the very reason he sold his shares to us as soon as he could, then split.

My sister guffaws as she cashes out a customer. "I'm sure. I bet it'd be awfully convenient if he could fix the leak between your legs too, huh?"

A vicious blush burns across my cheeks as I gape at her and a few of the chuckling guests. *Asshole.* She's always been that way. Straightforward and unfiltered. Even when we were kids, she loved making things awkward for me and Adrian any chance she could.

I open and close my mouth twice before narrowing my eyes. "I'll be on the top floor, working in the far wing. Call if you need something."

Willow chuckles, jerking her head to the man seated at the end of the bar. "See how she didn't deny my claims, Tommy?"

One of our long-time guests pats his round belly and grins my way. "I did, and now you got the poor girl running to the top floor."

"Oh, yeah, because the third floor is so high up there. We'll still be able to hear her journal entries from here. Dear diary, today Adrian did—"

"You are such a cunt, Will," I hiss through my teeth, twirling on my heels, my hands gripping the clipboard so tight it squeaks under the pressure.

"I have one, and I like to lick them, but I'm not one, Sam. Have fun upstairs!" my sister calls after me, and I have to *really* fight the urge not to flip her off.

Her need for a reaction out of me has been an ongoing battle since fifth grade when I swore on a pinky promise I didn't like-like Adrian. She knows I lied on it and refuses to let me live it down.

Winding through the tight crowd, I exit the bar and enter the lobby. From the looks of it, you'd think it wasn't attached to one of the most popular pubs on the block. It's empty of anyone except the receptionist and bellboy huddled across the wide counter.

When my parents renovated, they kept a lot of the detail and original lighting, but some things had to be redone to help modernize the place a bit. The check-in counter and doors have the original dark oak, while the gold metal accents have been restored to their previous shine. But things like the horrendous wallpaper and dingy carpets were replaced.

Overall, I really like how it somehow mixes both worlds. Cozy yet elegant. Historic yet contemporary.

I wave to the pair as I pass by and walk to the elevator on the left, then head to the top floor. Because the parade is on the east side of the building, the west is completely vacant. The rooms are booked with check-ins starting in a few hours, but for now, it will be a guest interruption-free zone while I work.

The long hall is similar to the lobby, sporting the rejuvenated original hardware, elaborate crown molding, and vintage sconces and chandeliers, but has also been given a modern feel as well. The walls are snowy gray, the doors dark oak, and the carpets a deep red.

I check over my list as I walk to the nearest maintenance closet. There's one on each floor, so we don't have to haul stuff up constantly. Deciding on running through the smaller jobs first, I grab my electrical bag and get started.

An hour later, I've managed to fix three loose light fixtures, two beeping smoke detectors, one crooked keyless entry, and four janky toilet flushers. I mean, I'm feeling insanely proud of myself, if I'm honest. Saved about a thousand bucks already, considering what the locals are charging right now, and barely broke a sweat.

See, I don't need Adrian, I internally snap at my sister as I move down to the next room on my list, 3T. My eyes flash to my list and I stop mid-step.

Dammit. Instant karma has to be the worst possible thing. Or perhaps the wicked bad energy I know my sister is pushing through the floors. Either way, I'm now pouting because this is the room with the bad sink.

The sink that haunts my freaking nightmares. It has a

mysterious leak no one can seem to find, and even with replacing the plumbing underneath *twice*, it still drips.

With a heavy sigh, I unlock the door, prop it open, and haul my large bag inside. Unlike the typical hotels, our rooms open to a small living area with two chairs around a fireplace. It's an electric built-in, but it gives the illusion of a vintage vibe. Behind the seating is the king-sized bed, and on the right is the door to the bathroom. It's an odd setup, considering if the door is open, you have a direct view of the stand-in shower, but it hasn't seemed to pose a problem thus far.

I drop my heavy tool bag on the floor outside of the bathroom and prop the door open. Inside, the perpetrating sink rests inside a beautifully refinished wooden cabinet with iron claw feet. Kneeling, I swing the doors open and expose the plumbing. Naturally, the little bowl I placed beneath last week is a quarter of the way full, and a droplet is growing heavy at the bottom of the pipe.

After turning off the pipe, I make quick work of emptying the bowl, cleaning the bottom, and throwing on gloves. My plan is to take out all the parts, put water in each one, and hope that I see something. If not, I'll seal it with new plumber's tape and will have to figure something out after the holiday rush.

I grab my trusty, adjustable pliers and get to work on the pipe. Normally, the pipes are a pain in the ass to loosen, but I guess today I'm due an extra workout, because no amount of turning is doing anything to budge it.

Deciding to readjust, I get on my knees and use both hands now, yanking with small bursts of energy. Having to run up and down the hotel, I'd say I'm a pretty in-shape person, with great stamina. But the way I'm currently struggling for air as I fight the sink, has me considering just how in-shape I really am.

Again, I yank, this time with a frustrated growl, hoping it will give me some type of extra testosterone. But instead, my grip slips from the pliers, and I fall back awkwardly, hitting a very hard... person.

Before I even look up, I feel the burn lighting up my entire face, but when I see familiar hazel eyes and black tousled hair, I beg for the floor to collapse altogether.

"Hey, Adrian," I breathe.

"Hey, Sammy."

Samantha

CHAPTER TWO

I'm pretty sure embarrassment is supposed to fly out the window when you do something like fall on your ass in front of your best friend. The one who's also witnessed me being stuck in an air duct, eating chocolate until I'm nearly sick after being stood up on a date, and sees me on FaceTime when I'm still half asleep, looking like a rag doll. But with the lingering, misplaced feelings I've yet to truly shake, it doesn't. So not only is my body burning from the humiliation, but my core aches from the intense clench.

Mainly due to his smile.

Like everything else about the man, it's sexy as sin, including the slightly larger canines, completing my Twilight fantasies. Team Jacob or Edward, it doesn't really matter when they both can chase down their prey and tear them to shreds. *Swoon.*

Adrian leans down and grips me firmly by the shoulders before titling me forward. With my heart beating in my throat, I latch on to the counter and carefully hoist myself to my feet.

"Having a bit of trouble with Doris?" He gestures to the sink, threading one hand through his hair while the other disappears inside his jean pocket. The white Henley hugging his massive frame leaves nothing to the imagination, but instead,

showcases the hours he spends ramming into other guys on the field.

Somehow, I feign annoyance and roll my eyes as I rip the gloves from my hands, and brush invisible dust from my slacks. "I don't know why you and Willow named this infernal thing."

He chuckles, and I instantly wish he hadn't. The sound is deep and gruff. "Because you have to talk to these things and be gentle with them. Something like handyman foreplay, so you loosen them up."

I try my best not to notice the way his words make my insides tingle and shove the pliers into his solid chest. "By all means."

Adrian's warm hand brushes against mine as he accepts the tool with a sly smile. "Nice to see you, too."

"Don't try to make me feel like an ass. I literally saw you on FaceTime before your game to wish you luck."

He throws an arm casually around one of my shoulders and *side* hugs me, like a decade-old friend *should*. Still, the pang in my chest is hard to ignore. "Because I lose any game when I don't get to talk to you beforehand. Look, I'll take care of Doris, and you can go work on the rest of your list. Then, we're getting drinks, since I haven't been home in two weeks."

I scoff and shove his arm off playfully, like my stomach isn't experiencing a tsunami from the massive butterfly frenzy. "Yeah, if you get that thing to go leak-free for more than three minutes, drinks are on me."

Adrian holds out a big hand. "Yeah?"

Reluctant at his confidence, but also sure Doris is the literal worst and won't stop leaking for anyone, I shake. "Deal."

It's funny how I don't get jittery or nervous when our hands touch. Believe it or not, it's actually calming.

"Good luck," I mutter as I grab the few things I'll need to finish the rest of the hall.

He smirks, pushing up his sleeves and revealing thick, tan forearms. Something about it feels dangerous as hell. "Ah, Bambi. You know anytime you wish me luck, I never fail."

"Yeah, yeah. We'll see." I quickly turn around, desperate to get some air not flooded with his warm scent. It's a mix of things I've never been able to describe but reminds me of the Venus flytrap. Pleasant and alluring, waiting for its prey to hop in its lap.

With a dismissive wave, I hurry to the next room and continue with the myriad of things on my list, all while ignoring the damned butterflies.

Thirty minutes later, my first list is complete. My arms are killing me, and my hands are covered in black soot from one of the air vent closets, but everything is done and ready for guests. The second list can wait till my body isn't bordering on collapse.

I trail back to room 3T, and find that no matter how much I readied myself to see Adrian, I'm never truly prepared.

He's on his back with his shirt off. Sweat glistens across his muscles and glides down the dips and valleys of each one. They contract every time he rotates his hand to tighten the trap into place.

Heavy grunts echo in the small space and collide with my libido, weakening my knees and forcing me to lean into the threshold. The effect as frustrating as always, and I make a mental note to scroll on Tinder later to distract me.

With a dramatic sigh that does little to drown out his

groans, I kick his bent knee. "I know you said foreplay, but this is a little much, Adrian."

His laugh fills the air as he draws himself out of the cabinet. "We'll see if you have that same condescending tone when you realize she's fixed."

I scoff. "Yeah, right."

"See for yourself." He gestures to the plumbing, but when his eyes drop over my frame, my breath stalls.

For a moment, I assume he's assessing the mess I'm sporting from the stupid air vent, but the way his eyes darken and linger say something else entirely. His tongue peeks out, sweeping across his lips as his gaze moves upward, and by the time he meets my eyes, I'm flushed and barely pulling in air.

Then, just as quickly as everything became dense, he smiles and speaks in a casual tone that makes me feel like I've imagined the entire thing. "Right now, you remind me of that time you got yourself all dirty. What did I used to call you back then?"

He pauses, as if he really needs to think about it while I'm already cringing at the memory. "It was Stinky Sam."

Adrian snaps his fingers. "That's right. After you fell into the mud."

"First of all, you pushed me into the mud. Second, this is dust."

He takes a step forward, a grin planted firmly on his face. "We were wrestling, and you *lost*."

"Because I *lost* focus. You were acting like you–" I stop myself, snapping my mouth shut. It's enough to be reminded of the one time I tried to make a move, only to be shoved not only into the friend zone, but into actual mud as well.

He takes another step, and my pulse begins to quicken. His voice lowers. "Acting like what?"

I shake my head, forcing my chin up to meet his gaze. He

knows what I'm talking about. We were eleven, and at the park, while our parents fumigated a hall. We were in the woodsy spot because the trails were boring, playing a classic game of tag. It had rained that week and there were plenty of mud puddles I was having trouble avoiding, considering I'm more on the clumsy side.

Naturally, Adrian caught me and had me pinned with nowhere to go, but still, I tried to duck away. He allowed me the brief courtesy of diving under his arms, but then snatched me around the waist and twirled me around. We ended up on the ground and began wrestling, not uncommon for us on a Tuesday. But somehow, I managed the delightfully rare scenario of ending up on top of him like Nala in the Lion King.

I yelled out my victory in time to be tossed on my back with him hovering over me like a predator about to rip their prey to shreds. But even with the thought of possibly being devoured, I never felt so alive. My heart was pounding, my nerves were on fire, and the excitement between us was palpable.

But then he ruined everything. His eyes did the thing you'd see in movies before a guy kissed the girl, and for a second—the sweetest second—my crush wasn't one-sided.

I closed my eyes and puckered. I freaking *puckered.*

Luckily, Adrian has always been a nice guy, even in fifth grade, and let me down easy. He rolled to the side, and suddenly aware of what was happening, I moved too, only right into the mud. I drenched myself in both filth and humiliation that day.

He helped me up, but gave me the name Stinky Sam, permanently etching in stone that we would never be more than friends. We've never talked about or even passively brought it up. So I guess there's that.

"Acting like what, Sam?" Adrian's voice is closer now,

plucking me from my thoughts and into the realization he is only a few inches from me.

His broad frame blocks the bathroom light, casting us in a dark shadow. Just like when we were kids, his lids are lowered, his face tilted, as if he plans to close the distance. My heart hammers in my chest, and a heaviness blooms low in my core, only this time, I don't make the same idiotic mistake.

Instead, I push out a breath and my words. "You know like what."

"I don't think I do." His tone is low, and husky.

I'm pretty sure at this point he can see the vein pulsing in my neck, but still, I'm able to steel my voice as I say what we've ignored for over fifteen years. "Like you were going to kiss me."

Adrian's eyes flash to my lips, then back up. "Would you have let me?"

"What?" I'm not sure the words are audible until he shifts his weight and moves forward.

"I'm curious. Would you have let me?"

Adrian isn't the one to play wicked games, not when it comes to people's feelings, so the notion he's asking, with his lips three inches from mine, almost feels like a dream. Or a nightmare waiting to rear its head.

"Of course not. Why do you ask?"

His lips pull down in the corners, and he shrugs, backing away casually as if he wasn't just suffocating me with want. "Only wondering, Bambi."

Adrian snatches the shirt from the counter before gesturing to the sink again. "Now, have a look so you can buy me that drink."

CHAPTER THREE

M y Stinky Sam.

Most people don't know this, but fear can be smelled as easily as it can be seen. It seeps into the pheromones and releases through sweat. It triggers a heightened response in the brain of those that smell it, and my Bambi smells fucking delicious.

The heavy arousal and excitement that flows from her anytime we're around each other is both intoxicating and addicting. So much so, in fact, that I almost slipped up. Almost gave in to the powerful urges I always have to fight against.

Hell, if she would have said yes when I asked her if she'd let me kiss her back then, I don't think anything could have stopped me from giving in and taking her now.

And I want to. So. Fucking. Bad.

Have for so long, I don't remember a time I didn't. Unfortunately, it isn't just the fact I'm nervous we'd mess up our friendship if we pursued what obviously streams between us. Though in all honestly, I think we're perfect for one another.

We share many commonalities while challenging each other when we can. Our conversations flow easily, and we usually don't go long without laughing. We fit in all ways two people can, except perhaps one.

It's my... rough nature, I'm worried about.

My needs and desires to be dominant and give in to very primitive and carnal urges are something I don't think my sweet Bambi would like.

Any man I've seen her date is generally softer in nature, the suit type, and doesn't know which direction north is without a phone.

I'm much different from that. I'm all hard edges and only wear suits when our team is required to attend a dinner. I thrive in nature, both physically, and well, sexually. I'm not sure when it happened. When a game of tag became a need to hunt. When finding Sam felt like catching prey. Or when the adrenaline turned into exhilaration and arousal.

But now, it's part of who I am–a part I need. And not knowing if Sam will accept that is enough to make me keep her at arm's length.

For now, at least.

Samantha bends at the knee and checks under the cabinet. Her loose ponytail has fallen, spilling over her soiled white blouse. Forbidden visuals flash through my mind, and it takes too long for me to reel them in.

Flushed skin. Quick breathing. Trembling on the edge. *Fuck.*

"I'm not sure if I should be happy or irritated. I've had more than enough people look at this damn sink, and you fixed it in less than an hour." She stands back up and crosses her arms, those big brown eyes glimmering with annoyance.

I shrug casually, tossing my shirt back on. "A thank you will suffice. Oh, and that drink."

She huffs. "Yeah, yeah. Tell Willow they're all on the house."

"You tell her. You're coming with me."

Sam shakes her head, lifting her clipboard. "Still have lots to do and—"

The cell phone ringing in her pocket cuts her off. She digs it out and blows out a breath before answering. "What's up?"

She listens for a response and shifts her eyes from me to scowling at the sink, then to herself in the mirror. Her brows shoot up, and her mouth drops as she takes in her disheveled appearance.

Dark dust covers the bridge of her nose and near her hairline, where she must have wiped her face. Her blouse is just as dirty, and the way her hair is barely held in place by the band, makes it appear as though she's just got done wrestling.

Little does she know how utterly gorgeous she looks right now.

"Alright, let me get changed, and I'll be right down." Sam taps the red button before slipping her phone back into her pocket and glaring at my reflection in the mirror. "Why didn't you tell me I looked this bad?"

I wave her off and answer honestly. "You look fine to me. Besides, you're up here working. Did you expect to stay pristine?"

"Presentable at least." She's fussing with her hair now, running her fingers through it in an attempt to comb out the tangles.

"What's wrong with getting a little dirty? Shows a job well done."

Her brown eyes flash to mine briefly, and for a moment, I wonder if she hears the undercurrent message in my words.

God, what I would give to see her drenched in sweat, riddled with leaves and streaks of dirt, marked by my mouth.

My cock twitches in my jeans, the imagery adding more than I can handle right now. When I glance back at her, I realize I must be wearing an expression that gives some type of insight into my thoughts because a blush has crept across her nose, and her breathing is louder.

I grin, trying my best to act unbothered–unphased by her natural reactions that sing to my urges. "I can help finish some of the things on your list if you'd like. Meet you downstairs in a bit."

She's silent for a moment before turning around and propping her hands on the sink at her side. "I mean, if you don't mind. I didn't plan on doing it till after the rush, but it would be nice to just have it done."

"Of course." I take the clipboard from her and scan over a few lines. None of it is too tedious and shouldn't take longer than an hour. "This is still my home, even if my name isn't on it anymore."

Sam smiles softly, the skin creasing near her eyes. "If you insist, I won't object. How long are you here for?"

"A couple of weeks. The next two games are close by."

"Oh, nice." Her bottom lip disappears between her teeth. "So you'll be around to bother me?"

I lift my hand with the full intent to tug her lip free, but with the tension already so thick, I decide to grant us both some much needed relief. When I ruffle her hair, an annoyed laugh erupts from her mouth as she pushes me off.

"I'll take that as a yes."

Nodding, I clean up the supplies on the floor. "Yep. So make sure my spot on the couch is free."

Sam rolls her eyes, handing me the clipboard. "Sorry, but Bell has taken a liking to your 'spot'. She owns it now."

"Good thing I like that cat. Guess your spot is mine now."

Her nose scrunches up like a little mouse. "My ass. There are plenty of other cushions to choose from."

I lower my gaze, unable to control the lust from seeping into my words. It's becoming harder to keep myself in check around her. "It's mine now, Bambi."

Her throat bobs with a thick swallow before she regains some type of composure. That's when a sexy, defiant type of smirk lifts one side of her lips. "If you think you have a right to claim it, by all means, you can have it."

Now it's my turn to be surprised. My pulse increases as she spins on her heels and exits the bathroom. My every instinct is to grab her, throw her on the bed and claim her now, but the heavy truth of why I don't, anchors my feet in place.

No matter how much we tread the line, it's better this way. Safer. Because the illusion of the possibility is better than knowing the truth–I can never have her. Not in the ways I want.

But as hard as it is, it's okay. Her friendship is worth more. Her genuine love and support are more than enough. I'm lucky to have her in my life at all, let alone being my closest friend.

"Hurry up and come down when you're done. I'll need saving from Willow," Sam says over her shoulder.

Forcing my eyes on the paper she left behind, I chuckle nonchalantly. "That'll cost you a buddy shot."

Her laugh echoes down the hallway with words I never thought I'd hear. "Yes, sir. Whatever you say."

Oh, Bambi. If only.

CHAPTER FOUR

What the hell was that about?

Heading to the room at the end of the hall-way, I fail for the third time to control my racing heart. Adrian and I have always been close, and very comfort-able with each other. There have been countless times we've laid on each other's laps, gotten changed in the same room, and hell, even slept in the same bed. And while all those occasions have been borderline torturous to both my heart and libido, never have we crossed the line into *clear* flirting.

I wouldn't even call that flirting. Honestly, it was more like ripping our clothes off and finally giving in to a feeling we both have always wanted. Both. Plural. Not just me. For a moment, I felt crazy, like I was imagining him coming on to me, but then there was only validation.

There was no question there was a shift in the air. The tension was so thick, it was hard to breathe through it. The desire in his eyes was so undeniable, I could guarantee that if I kissed him, it would have finally led to something.

But I didn't–I *couldn't*–because somewhere deep down, I'm scared. Scared of foregoing his friendship and what we have. And *nothing* is worth losing that. Not even proving to myself it isn't all in my head.

I unlock the door we use as a spare room. Willow and I pass out here occasionally when we work too late, or we happen to get too drunk after a long night of celebrating Adrian's recent victory. The locals always convince us to play a game where we have a shot every time he scores or sip a drink when he knocks a guy on his ass.

Naturally, we always end up completely hammered.

Inside, I hop in the shower and change into some of the spare clothes we leave here. I ignore the fact that I grab a black lace bra and matching panties, then quickly get myself together before rushing downstairs.

Willow called and said she was slightly overwhelmed and needed the barbacks to start taking orders, which means I need to fill in for them. One thing I've learned is while I'm great at fixing average maintenance issues, I am the worst bartender alive.

Ninety percent of the drinks I make will either have you drunk on the first sip or wondering if there is any alcohol in it at all.

When I make it back downstairs, I'm much calmer. My mind is finally clear of the fog and I'm able to focus on the massive amount of bodies in the pub.

I mentally send energy into the air that no fire marshals decide to pay us a visit as I excuse myself through the crowd. At the bar, my sister is rushing around behind it while her three barbacks cash people out.

She nods at me while pouring a round of shots. "We need clean glasses, bottles restocked, and the ice bin refilled."

I narrow my eyes and tilt my head.

Willow groans as she slams down her bottle and slides the small glasses toward waiting hands. "Alright, sorry about what I said earlier. Can you please help your big sister out?"

I purse my lips, half inclined to make her grovel a little

more, but decide not to push my luck. She'll only retaliate later, and with Adrian staying for a while this time, I don't want to make things more awkward than they need to be.

Still, I have to ask one thing before agreeing to be an errand girl. "Did you tell Adrian where I was?"

She smirks, accepting a hundred-dollar bill from the young patron. "Answer this first. Why are you fresh out of the shower?"

My mouth pops open, a blush burning up my neck. "Because I got dirty from the damn vent closet on third. You know we need to get it cleaned."

"And there isn't any other reason?"

Tommy, still sitting in his same spot, shifts and eyes me up and down. After a thoughtful pause, he turns back to my sister. "Be nice to your kid sister, Willy. And to be fair, I don't think she'd be standing so straight if Adrian finally made a move."

"Tommy!" my sister and I yell out in unison, but he merely shrugs.

Annoyed with both of them, I stomp off in the direction of the storage unit behind the bar. The entire time I work around my sister and the barbacks, I try to drown out my heart racing in my ears, and the memories of me and Adrian in the bathroom.

I empty out the four trash bins and replace the bags. *He was just being friendly.*

I fill up the two ice buckets and dump them into the reservoirs. *He's being a good friend and helping out.*

I replenish the empty shelves, wipe down the counters, and haul the dishes to the back. *He doesn't look at you like that. He's your best friend, for fuck's sake.*

Around the third tray of dishes I push into the washer, my sister appears in the back. She juts her thumb toward the door to the bar. "Parade's about to start, so it's quieted down. You're off the hook."

My shoulders fall in relief. "Oh, thank goodness. I was about two seconds away from collapsing."

Willow grunts. "It wasn't that bad."

I wave my wrinkling fingers in her face. "I'm a hundred-year-old prune right now."

She rolls her eyes, but a sincere smile curls her lips. "Seriously, though, thank you. I knew it'd get busy before the parade, but damn. I called in a few more people to help with the night shift."

Yanking off my apron, I toss it to her. "Even better. I'm about to go upstairs and take the longest nap of my life."

"So what should I tell Adrian?"

This stops me, and my pulse increases. "What do you mean?"

She shrugs. "He texted me that he's about done with the list you gave him and wants to know if he can grab the key to the spare room, so he can shower before he meets you for drinks."

I draw my lip through my teeth, debating how badly I want the nap. Finally, I decide against it and shake my head. "It's fine. Go ahead and give it to him, and I'll go fiddle around in the ballroom to get ready for Monday's event."

Her light brows furrow. "We have all weekend to worry about that."

"Yeah, but I have nothing better to do."

"How about taking a nap?"

"I don't want to disturb–"

"Okay, stop with the bullshit." My sister's hands find her hips, and I internally groan, knowing a lecture is on the horizon. "He's literally walked around half-naked before. Taken a shower at our place while we cooked breakfast. Changed his clothes as if we weren't in the room. I mean, the list goes on. So why would you being in the same room while he showers be any different than any of those times?"

"It's not."

"Yet you're acting weird about it. Did something happen?" Her voice is lower now, taking on a serious edge. "Spill it."

Lying to my sister is futile, has been since I attempted to do so when pinky swearing in fifth grade. She says I have a tell, and has always been able to sniff out any crap I try to sell her.

Still, I try. "Nope."

Willow's lips lift into an eerie smile. *Dammit.*

"Try again, baby sister."

"Why does it matter?"

"Because it's about making a point."

I mirror her stance and toss my hands on my hips. Can't beat them, deflect. "And what point would that be?"

"You suck at lying and you're crazy in love with Adrian."

My eyes hurt from flaring so wide, but I try my hand at annoyance. "Are you still on about that? It's been fifteen years, Will."

"And it's about damn time you admit you lied. On a pinky swear, no less. It's the principle."

"You're such an igit."

She throws her head back as laughter tumbles past her lips. "An igit who's right. You don't want to admit it? Fine. But don't insult me as your sister and friend by lying about why you can't take a damn nap around him."

There's something I both hate and love about having my sister also be my best friend. While I can tell her about the horrendous dates I have with the boring tax attorney, or my secret desire to be railed like a complete whore by the guy who plays Winter Soldier, I filter anything that pertains to Adrian.

24

It's mainly because he's also Willow's friend. I'd hate for her to make things more awkward, or even worse, feel the need to stop hanging around us altogether.

But the look on her face does things to make me feel like a crappy sister.

Freaking jerk.

"You love making me feel like an ass."

"Isn't it my job?"

Throwing my hands up in defeat, I give her a general synopsis of what happened in the bathroom. I explain how it felt like I was imagining things, but at the same time, I know I wasn't. How I'm both confused and nervous about the shift in the air. That there's something different.

She leans against the threshold of the door, looking out at the bar for a moment as she digests what I've said. What I've pretty much admitted. When she turns back around, I'm surprised by the genuine earnestness in her voice.

"He's losing his will to keep you at arm's length."

I lift a questioning brow. "And that means?"

Willow sighs, redoing her ponytail that's come slightly loose. "He's fighting the same urges you are. Probably worried about ruining a twenty-year-old friendship for a night in the sack."

I swallow around the thick lump suddenly in my throat. When she doesn't elaborate, I clear my throat. "You're saying what?"

"I think it's pretty obvious he wants you just as bad, Sam. But naturally, he's holding back like you are. Seems like it's getting harder for him, though. My advice?"

I nod, and she straightens. "Be an adult and confront it. If you both communicate, you might be surprised to find out how something that seems impossible is actually easy."

Chapter 4

Without another word, she pushes the swinging door open and disappears, leaving me with my heart in my throat and my mind full of what-ifs.

CHAPTER FIVE

A m I hiding out in the ballroom? Possibly.
Am I terrified of what my sister left lingering in the air? Yep.

What about the possibilities that could be if I had an adult conversation with Adrian, instead of letting it fall to the wayside because of some type of miscommunication? Also, a resounding yes. Absolutely petrified.

But will I allow myself to do anything about it? Honestly, I don't know.

I want to. I think.

For the second time today, I construct a mental list of the possible pros and cons that can happen if I were to outright tell Adrian I have feelings for him. That I have since forever and want to try to pursue things.

Pros: He feels the same, and we try it out.

Cons: I lose a dear friend. I mess up a three-way friendship that's been around since Google was founded. I potentially lose the best handyman the hotel has ever had.

Obvious weight leans on me, just keeping my mouth shut and trying to move on. Maybe what happened in the bathroom was a fluke. A misinterpreted moment of weakness when I was drowning in everything Adrian.

I do my best to ignore the squeezing sensation in my chest and slip out my phone as I walk to the piano. Flopping down on the hard bench, I press my back into the closed key cover and tap on the dating app.

For the next few minutes, I scroll through profiles and assess the men on the screen in less than five seconds. All of them the app matches me with are the exact same. Suits, ties, bright smiles, and perfectly uniform hair.

I tried this type before. Multiple times. And every time I go on a date, I always end up bored out of my mind. From the fancy restaurants, where we talk about their latest business venture to the missionary sex, where I never get off.

It starts and ends the same every single time. I need something exciting. Something that makes me feel alive.

Maybe then the lingering feelings will begin to dwindle. Maybe then I won't feel completely pathetic and can move on from what I've never even had.

As if on cue, the ballroom door opens, and I twirl around, ready to mouth off to Willow. Only it isn't my sister standing in the large doorway. It's freaking Adrian.

I hit the button on the side of my phone, before placing it face down on the piano. "All done?"

He's more disheveled than he was when he was working on Doris. His hair is tousled, falling over his forehead, while his Henley is no longer white, but is covered with an array of streaking grays, blacks, and browns. His jeans are low on his hips, sporting the same colors as his shirt.

Adrian nods, seemingly pleased with himself. "I am."

I stand up and move around the piano, but still leave plenty of room between the both of us. "Thank you, seriously."

He waves me off. "I told you, this is my home too. And you know it's never an issue helping you ladies out. Better me than some townie who's gonna overcharge you."

"Still. Thank you, Adrian."

He nods again as he lets his gaze drop to the instrument behind me. After a few seconds, he looks back to me.

"Remember when you got stuck in there." He gestures to the grand piano with his chin, a sly grin on his face.

Ignoring the unexpected swell of butterflies, I guffaw. "Of course. I thought it was the perfect hiding spot."

"If you *planned* on breaking the damn thing, sure."

I roll my eyes. "I definitely didn't intend to harm your precious piano. Just determined to finally win a game of hide and seek with you."

"Bambi, we both know you will never win a game with me. Wherever you hide, I will find you."

I bite into my bottom lip hard, an attempt to feel something other than the sudden ache in my core. "Sounds a bit stalkerish, but I get your meaning."

He shrugs, seemingly indifferent to the higher octave in my voice. "Not my fault you suck at hiding."

"Umm, I don't," I bite out, folding my arms over my chest. "You always cheat."

This makes him laugh that deep, throaty laugh. "How do I cheat, Sam?"

I mirror his shrug, though a little more aggressively. "I don't know. But there's no way you should have been able to find me every single time."

Adrian moves toward me slowly, each step in tune with slow-motion seconds in a movie. His gaze is hooded and predatory, his posture screaming for me to back up. Instead, I stand perfectly still, a strange response when my body is humming to do the opposite. But it isn't because I'm afraid. It's anticipation.

The closer he gets to me, the more my heart rate increases. The quicker my breath comes, the wetter I get. Scandalous, and so freaking forbidden, but it's the very excitement I go out looking for, which is making it very hard for me to ignore.

By the time Adrian is a foot away from me, my nerves are shaking in anticipation. "You know what I think, Sam? I think you like it when I chase you. And even more so when I find you."

I force my lids to lower, an attempt to be unphased. But my voice is too breathy, and the way his eyes flash to my neck tells me he can see my raging pulse. Still, I try. "Something tells me you like it just as much. If not more."

"And if I do?"

My mind races, thoughts of what my sister said flashing through one by one. But only one of those stands out.

"Be an adult and confront it. If you both communicate, you might be surprised to find out how something that seems impossible is actually easy."

I swallow, but it gets stuck in my throat. My eyelashes flutter as I choke in the moment. Fear of saying the wrong thing grips me too tight to speak.

A flash of resignation appears in Adrian's eyes before he steps back, chuckling. "You should have seen your face, Bambi. Like a deer in headlights. I was messing with you."

My stomach turns with his words. Embarrassment and naivety swirling around in my gut.

When I don't say anything, he yawns. "I only came down to tell you I'm done, and I'm going to take a long shower. We still on for drinks?"

I manage to nod a quick yes, and the smile slowly fades on his face.

"Look, sorry about earlier, and now. The flight really must have done a number on me. I think I need some rest."

His slight admission to the clear shift is slightly reassuring.

It informs me I'm not losing my fucking mind with what I've been feeling this afternoon. "No worries. Probably jetlag."

"Yeah. Probably. I'll let you get back to your Tinder." Like my sister, he doesn't wait for a response and exits the ballroom.

For the first time in my life, I want to slap myself on the forehead. I'm a grown-ass woman. Adrian is my closest fucking friend. We talk about everything from the day-old yogurt I found in between my couch cushions one time, to that one occasion he had film in his belly button.

Yet I can't open my mouth and be like, *"Hey, I like you more than a friend. Want to fuck me?"*

A horrific grunt burns my nostrils as I return to the piano bench, shame coating my insides in something grimy. In an attempt to forget about it, I open Tinder again and lose myself in the slew of men it matches me with.

After a few more minutes of scrolling left on the app, my eyelids grow heavy. I've done a lot, and with the influx coming tonight, I know I'll benefit from lying down, even if I don't get to sleep long. By now, I suspect Adrian is probably already in the shower. They are notoriously thirty minutes long, which is actually the perfect amount of time for a power nap.

Heading back up to the spare room, I talk myself off a ledge.

Things are fine.

It's been a weird day.

A long week.

I haven't seen him in a while, and we're both pretty tired.

Everything is normal.

I just need a few minutes of sleep.

When I unlock the door, I open it with my redundant thoughts still playing on a loop. I don't notice the bathroom door wide open. I don't notice the tan muscles moving under the stream of water. Nor do I don't notice the grunts of pleasure.

Until I do.

Holy shit.

Adrian is facing me, one hand above his head, clasped on the top of the glass shower door, while the other is down low, gripped around his massive erection. My body responds immediately, tightening and tingling, as I take in his form. His clenched abs. His flexing muscles. His dick. Fuck, why is it so damn thick?

Stop it.

Somewhere deep, my consciousness is able to scream above my arousal and tell me to turn around. To have some freaking decency and let my best friend masturbate in peace. To leave and just wait for him at the bar.

But the little voice in my head is fading. She's drowning under the steady slaps of water as he works his hand up and down his thick shaft. It's fading into the background the moment his groans of pleasure reach my ears.

The muscle in his jaw tics as his hand moves faster, his head falling into the crook of his arm with the increased speed.

My pussy aches, clenching around nothing as I bear witness to the sexiest thing I've ever seen in my life.

I should leave.

I shouldn't be turned on.

My hand sure as hell shouldn't be lingering at the waistband of my pants, my fingers trailing along my lower stomach, sprouting goosebumps in their wake.

What is wrong with me?

I bite down on my lip and spin on my heels to leave. But the moment I touch the doorknob, one singular word stops my movement. It rocks my world and tears down everything I thought I knew.

It changes *everything.*

It's a heady moan, full of lust not even I can misconstrue. And when he says it again, I come undone.

"Samantha."

Adrian

CHAPTER SIX

Maybe I was wrong.

Maybe the only thing holding me back from letting down my guard and really pursuing Sam was me.

I watched her deny at least twenty guys on that app, and each one appeared to be the same flavor, just in a different colored suit. Perhaps she's bored, like I was before I figured it out. Before I realized the things I needed to make me feel like me.

It's clear in the way she responds to me–her body's natural reactions.

Her big doe eyes, her throbbing pulse, the pungent scent of fear and want, wafting in the air. Sam wants the excitement.

She craves it.

Which could mean she may very well desire what I have to give.

My heart swells in my chest, the idea that things don't have to be a desire but could be a reality, making my blood soar.

Tonight, I'll make it happen. Find a way to tell her everything. *Show* her everything, and then go from there. It's been daunting to be lost in what-ifs, what could bes, and maybes. At least after tonight, I'll know.

We both will.

I unlock the door to the spare room. There were plenty of times we had to have sleepovers up here while our parents worked late into the night. Most of the time, we would stuff ourselves with popcorn and watch the latest Disney channel movie, or play board games. On some occasions, after Willow fell asleep, or got lost in her phone, talking to her latest girl-friend, Sam and I would wander the halls.

We'd look into the few rooms yet to be renovated and talk about what we imagined happened in the past. The types of people who would come stay here. We'd even come up with stories when we found little knickknacks.

One of the last times we searched the rooms, Sam tripped and fell hard into an old dresser. She's always been a little clumsy, but that was the day she solidified the "Bambi" nick-name. I laughed after helping her up and used it for the first time.

"Come on, Bambi, get yourself together."

Her brown eyes flare before she chucks something small and round at my face. "Shut up. The carpets are crumpled. You should have caught me."

A heavy rock of guilt drops into my stomach as I bend to pick up the object. It's a dainty gold ring. Plain without all the frills, but on the inside, a script runs across the band.

My lucky charm.

"You're right, Sam." I take a step toward her and pull her soft hand toward me. She stands perfectly still, her shuddered breathing the only sound in the room. I slip the ring onto her thumb and twirl it around. "A promise to always catch you when you fall. Both physically and in life. My best friend to the end."

I winced when I heard my own words out loud, but she didn't seem to notice or care. She was all bright smiles and batting eyelashes. Her aura lit me up from the inside and her response fueled my decision to follow dreams I shoved away as just that–dreams.

"And as your best friend, I promise to always support anything you do. I know you were meant for bigger things outside of these walls, and I'm excited to be standing on the side- lines, cheering you on."

With a weary sigh, I turn on the water. She still wears the ring. It's on the middle finger of her right hand. Not once have I ever seen her take it off, which, in a way, irritates me more when I truly consider what it could mean.

I should have trusted her with this part of my life sooner. Saved myself the torture of wondering what we would be like. What we'd *really* be like.

After testing the water, I step inside and try to force my body to relax. To not think of everything that's happened today. But the more I try to empty my thoughts, the harder I have to work.

To be honest, I'm only so strong when it comes to Sam. Always have been. It's the only part I like about having to leave for games and training–the forced space. It gives me time to breathe, to not overwhelm myself with wanting to forgo my fears and fall into her.

The hot water pelts into my tight muscles. I expect the pent-up tension to begin melting, but when it doesn't, I attempt to focus on the heat. On the way the warm droplets glide over my back and down my legs.

It isn't enough.

Nothing is enough anymore. I need a release. A moment of peace. Even if just for a second. *Fuck.*

With a fleeting admission, I give in to the blood soaring through my body and drop one hand to the base of my cock and lift the other to grab the top of the shower door. It's hard, pulsing angrily under my fingertips from the multiple times I've put myself in teasing situations with Sam today.

Starting slowly, I move my hand up and down, closing my eyes against the instant pleasure. Visions of Sam's long brown hair appear–it's whipping in the wind as she runs through the woods, her feet moving her in and out of the cluster of trees.

The beast in my chest rears its head, spiking my adrenaline so high I feel my pulse in the tips of my ears. My hand moves faster as I envision closing the space between us.

She's easy to catch, and even easier to subdue. I have her on the soft forest floor in seconds, her clothes ripped from her body in another. My plan is to take my time and worship every inch of her. Because in reality, I wouldn't be sweet and slow. I wouldn't be able to stop myself.

I would fucking devour her.

"Samantha." Her name is a hiss through clenched teeth, the warm euphoric ball winding tight in my spine as I move my mouth down her stomach.

Her mouth parts while soft whimpers escape into the night air. Only the faint noises sound too clear. Too real.

I peel my eyes open to mere slits, and the visual that replaces my fantasy is surreal. Sam is standing at the door, her head leaning against the frame, her knuckles white from clenching the handle so tightly.

She's not moving but standing still as though she isn't sure if she heard what she thought she did.

My insides begin humming as I consider testing the limit. To see what she'll do when she knows without a shadow of a doubt I said it.

"Samantha." It's a husky whisper, but I know she hears me.

Her hand drops from the knob, and slowly, oh so fucking slowly, she turns to face me. Her eyes trail from the ground and across the floor until they move up my frame and stop on my lowered gaze. Steam has filled the small room, clouding the shower now, but I know she can make out where my hand is, how fast it's moving.

Sam's mouth parts, her lashes fluttering when we make eye contact. From here, I can see her jaw clamp down the moment the want hits her.

She only lasts a second longer before her eyes squeeze shut and she bites down on her lip so hard, I'm sure she's drawn blood. Rotating back around, she grabs onto the door handle but doesn't move to leave, just simply stands. Like she's waiting.

Oh, Bambi.

Lightning begins to unfurl in my back, the electricity burning through my limbs as my orgasm comes. It barrels through me, and I have to bite into my raised arm to dull the roar vibrating my chest into a muffled growl.

By the time my eyes find Sam, her forehead is pressed against the door, her thighs pressed together. It winds me up all over again, and in a split second, I make the decision.

Fuck waiting.

I push the glass open and grab my towel, but in the next blink, the front door to the room is open and Samantha is stumbling over herself, a whispered, "Sorry" floating behind her.

Samantha

CHAPTER SEVEN

"I need a drink. Strong, please."

I nearly hurl myself onto the only empty barstool next to Tommy. The bar has begun to fill up again, but with the nighttime parade, it's still a manageable crowd.

He and my sister exchange a quizzical look before Willow finally drops a shot glass in front of me. "So, I'm guessing the talk didn't go so well?"

The guilt in her voice is so thick I almost want to lie and bask in the rarity of it. But the confusion and shock whirling around in my system are already more than I can handle.

She overpours her hand as she gapes at me, causing some of the liquor to seep over the side. I snatch the shot and down it quickly, relishing the burn as it radiates down my esophagus, burning away any words I had to explain what the fuck just happened.

The glass bounces as I slam it back down and nod my head for a refill. "Did you know a Shamrock is a three-leaf clover and was once called a 'seamroy'? It was a sacred plant that was a visual–"

"Representation of the Holy Trinity. Yeah, we know." My sister fills the shot glass again, before leaning across the counter. "What's wrong?"

I shake my head so fast, little spots decorate my vision. "What about that the first-ever St. Patrick's Day parade held in America was right here in Boston?"

This time, Tommy nods and lifts his beer mug. "In 1737."

Willow blows out an annoyed breath, but I ignore her and take back the second shot. "It's why we named the hotel, The Four Leaf. Our parents signed the lease on St. Paddy's Day and thought it was their good luck charm."

"That and they said it cost them a pot of gold to buy the damn place," Willow tells Tommy. "Would you give us a minute?"

He holds up a hand and nods. "Got to go to the John anyway."

She smiles an appreciative thanks, before narrowing her eyes at me. "Samantha Rayn, tell me what happened. You are– oh my gosh, are you okay?"

It's only now I've realized I haven't eaten anything but the breakfast hoagie this morning. Which was over nine hours ago. My head is already fuzzy, but I think it's more from working on an empty stomach than it is the liquor just entering my gut.

"You have a snack back there?" I mutter, pushing the glass toward her with my index finger.

She scoffs, gesturing to one of her barbacks. His name is Klien. Such an odd name, though also unique. I remember him telling me it was German, and when I researched it, I thought it was ironic. It means little. He's almost as tall as Adrian, which for me means I have to tip my head almost the whole way back–

The double snap of my sister's fingers forces me to stop staring at Klien. "Sam. Answer me."

I blink twice, my brows furrowing as I try to recall her asking me something.

Willow blows out a hard, irritated breath. "I asked what you wanted to eat, ass."

"Well, I definitely don't want ass to eat." I smile, trying to lighten her snappy mood. But then I consider a song I once heard that gloried what a good tongue can do to the back door. "Well, I mean, not right now. I'd prefer something digestible."

"For fuck's sake." She turns to Klien, clearly exasperated. "A croissant, please. Butter on the side."

"Oh, that's my favorite." I sit up straight, my mouth already watering at the promise of food. "I hadn't realized how much I've done without eating. Also, why are you so crabby?"

"Because my relatively straightforward sister is acting like an elusive dingbat rather than facing her one fear head-on."

"Rude," I mutter, tracing the bar top's grain with my pinky.

"Tell me what happened between you and Adrian."

Heat blossoms across my cheeks as the mere mention of his name makes me recall what he did. What *I* did.

My feet were freaking stuck to the floor when he said my name. I couldn't help but turn around–see if he'd stop if he knew I was there. But he didn't.

He kept going, and I *stayed*. I listened to the whole ordeal while my pussy clenched so tight it hurt. Like physically ached from how badly I wanted to... give in?

I bite the inside of my lip too hard and wince when I taste the copper spread across my tastebuds.

The realization–the concrete evidence, finally settles in, sending goosebumps down my arms.

Adrian Stokes was masturbating to me. *Me*. His best friend.

What the fuck am I supposed to do with that? Are things about to be awkward as hell? Or do we dive right in and make out on the couch?

If I'm being honest, I never thought about the beginning of what would happen if it ever did. Only the middle. The good parts. The place where we're comfortable with each other and everything just flows. Never in the fragile space where I could do something clumsy and possibly drive him away.

Funny thing–in Irish Lore, St. Patrick was known for driving snakes out of Ireland.

"You're trying to deflect. I see your mind working on another Saint Patrick's Day fact as we speak."

I swipe my hands down my face before peering over my shoulder. Tommy still hasn't returned, and all the patrons are too engrossed in their own conversations to give us a second glance. When I turn back to Willow, her amber eyes are wide, and her head is tilted to the side dramatically as she waits for me to speak.

"Fine, but for once in your life, please, *please,* Willow, don't say anything."

She takes an extensive pause, and for the first time, I realize what a "pregnant pause" is. It's one that lasts abnormally long, and when you think it's supposed to end, it keeps going, building anticipation.

It makes me feel jittery, so I decide to perform a C-section. "Promise, now."

She holds her hands up before throwing a rag over her shoulder. "Alright, alright. I promise."

I hesitate, but not nearly as long as she did, before I give her a very quick play-by-play, revisiting some details I already told her earlier today. The tension, the obvious shift, the feelings, my fifteen-year-old lie, and then... the shower incident.

By the time I finish, I'm flushed all over again, and my heart is doing a weird palpitating thing. Meanwhile, Willow seems completely unbothered and maybe even a bit entertained. Her eyes are creased in the corner, and one side of her lips is curled.

She remains silent as my pulse rages on, accepting my snack from Klien and nodding to Tommy, who returns to his seat.

My knee bounces against the metal of my stool, the entire thing vibrating as my legs shake. She gives me a deep look before nodding slowly, pushing my plate of food toward me. When I don't move to touch it because of the anxiety gripping my limps, she finally speaks.

"As your older sister and the more *forward* of us two, I have to say I'm pretty damn proud."

"Proud?" I gawk, surprise sweeping through me.

"Yeah, I mean. I would have thought you would have run out with your tail between your legs."

I yank the plate closer and tear off a corner of the croissant, biting it a little too aggressively. "I'm not a prude, Will."

"Didn't say you were, but clearly, you're having a bit of trouble processing. You experienced a little more sexual liberation and you don't know what to make out of it. But let me ask you this..." She leans over the bar, narrowing her eyes as she draws closer. I suck in air and hold it, unsure what to expect.

"Did you like it?"

The air escapes as my lips part, my mind floating back to every sound and movement he made. The ache and desire coil low in my stomach, telling me just how *badly* I liked it. My voice is barely above a whisper. "Yes."

The loud pop of my sister slapping the countertop makes me and Tommy simultaneously jolt upright in our chairs. "Alright then, good. Because something tells me he likes more adventurous things than a little self-exploration."

I pinch off another piece of the croissant, slowing down enough to spread some of the butter across the top. When I pop it into my mouth, I really taste it this time, the flavor spreading

43

over my tongue and making my toes curl. Hmm... maybe that's the liquor. "What do you mean?"

Willow tends to a small group of men who approach the bar. "You've seen him on the field, Sam. I don't think you're going to get soft kisses and foot rubs."

"I'll lose the foot rubs?" Adrian has given me plenty of massages while lounging on the couch, and let me tell you something, I'd probably go mental if I never got another one of those.

She huffs, clearly annoyed as she pops the tops off each of the mens' beers. "You're such a ditz."

One of the guys wearing a pair of khakis and a tropical print shirt, leans over. Even close to the bar, I can smell the potent liquor seeping from his pores. He nudges me with his shoulder before clasping a strong hand over my wrist, and his smug sneer causes my stomach to curdle. "I can give you foot rubs, doll."

Maybe because I'm a tad inebriated or still teetering on low blood sugar, but the next few things happen in slow motion. My sister grabs an empty bottle from the bin under the bartop, her intent clear as she lifts it up, but in the next second, she smiles and drops it back into the disposal.

I assume it's because she sees I'm turning to tell the asshole to get his grubby paws off me, but instead, an ominous chill stops me before I get a word out.

"I'd like to see you manage such a feat after I break both your hands." Adrian's husky voice is deadly, shooting through my core and raising the fine hairs over my entire body.

The man's neck cracks when he whips his head around to look at Adrian, probably ready to say something he'd regret. But the moment he makes eye contact, it's clear he wants no part in whatever he sees raging in Adrian's eyes.

He mumbles a quick apology, but when he releases my arm, Adrian grabs his. "A proper apology is in order."

It isn't a request. It's a downright order. There's a frightening shift in the air, and the instant sheen across the guy's forehead lets me know he feels it too. His murky blue eyes flit to me. "I'm sorry I touched you. I-I should have politely *offered* to rub your feet."

My gaze flashes to Adrian's, who's looking at the spot on my arm where the guy was holding me. There's a fire and anger I've only ever seen on my TV when he's smashing into an opponent, and even then, it pales in comparison to right now.

My body hums its approval as I nod to the guy, keeping my eyes on Adrian. "Thank you. Enjoy the rest of your evening."

"Appreciate it," he replies, his voice tight with Adrian's lingering hold.

Another beat passes before Adrian releases him and lets him rejoin his friend who vanished the second he had his drinks.

"You didn't need to do that." I don't say it as loud as I intend to, my nerves still a jumbled mess. "He wasn't any–"

"No one touches you, Bambi. Not without your consent." Adrian nods to Willow, who smiles and starts making what I assume is his regular drink. He turns to the side and places one forearm on the bar and the other hand on the back of my chair. His hazel eyes burn a trail up my frame until he reaches my face, to which he grins. "And I'm the only one who gets to massage your feet."

Samantha

CHAPTER EIGHT

I s what just occurred one of the sexiest things that has ever happened to me? Yeah—well, second, if I take into account what transpired while he showered. But him laying claim to my feet is in the close running.

My heart is currently bruising my sternum, while my pelvic floor is sore from the number of times my pussy has performed involuntary kegels.

As if he can read my mind, Adrian flashes me a full set of bright teeth before winking and turning to Tommy, completely unaware of the storm of butterflies he's released.

How the hell those things still have wings after today is beyond me.

"Hey, man. How've you been?"

Tommy's spine straightens, his eyes sparkling like a cartoon character as he replies to Adrian, and soon enough, they're lost in conversation. It's not an uncommon thing when he comes around. He's Adrian Stokes, after all. Number twenty-four. The local hero and prodigy. The boy on TV that everyone knows and watched grow up.

Usually, I poke fun at being best friends with someone famous, but right now, I use the moment to catch my damn breath and flash a look at my sister.

She eyes me in her periphery, a knowing smirk on her face as she purposely avoids looking at me.

Asshat.

I know what she wants. For me to communicate with him. To not let my age-old fear of a second rejection bog me down. And I was rejected. That day, in the woods, right before I was covered in mud. It was a clear move on my part and to have him do that still bothers me. In truth, it also fuels the constant trepidation I have when even considering broaching the subject again. Even though things have clearly shifted, I'm still allowed to be nervous.

Right then, I decide, if something happens, it has to be him who makes the move. I don't plan to make it easy.

Willow slides Adrian the drink before venturing down the bar to tend to other guests, while I swivel and glance out the pub windows. The daytime parade went by while I was working upstairs, but as the pretty dusk colors surge into the light blue sky, a new crowd forms on the sidewalk.

Most of them have neon green glow stick necklaces, and a long ale in one or both hands. Everyone is dressed in dark colors–per the flyer–and soon, only the glowing paint, which will be squirted on them, will be visible in the night.

It's a pretty cool concept, and honestly, I'm surprised it took the city this long to accommodate a nighttime crowd.

"Want to go out and watch?" Adrian's soothing voice causes goosebumps to sprout along my arms.

I swallow and shake my head. "It will be getting busy soon. I need to be here to help."

"That's why you have a staff." He doesn't touch me, but I feel him move closer behind me. One big breath, and I know my shoulders will brush against his chest. Something about being so close, yet not, is intoxicating.

47

Chapter 8

Perhaps it's the anticipation of the possibility that's so exciting.

"Why'd you run from me, Sam?"

I suck in a breath, but it's too thin, forcing me to clear my throat. He's near my ear now, his warm breath tickling the fine hairs on top. I'm grateful he can't see my mouth open and close twice before I find the right words. "I wasn't meant to see that. It was an invasion of a very private moment."

I can hear the grin on his face as he speaks. "If you weren't meant to see it, don't you think I would have stopped?"

The ache in my pussy flares, and I have to force my eyes to squeeze shut as I steady my breath. I can't respond. Not only because I don't know what to say, but also because I need it to be him. He has to outright say what's happening.

What's *finally* happening.

After a torturous pause, he says it. "Are you bothered by the fact I have to think of you to come?"

Breathing becomes nonexistent. My nerves ignite, burning through my limbs and setting my skin on fire. Somehow, I manage to shake my head.

His rumble of approval sends a tremor down my spine. "After I finish this drink, I want to play a game with you, Sam. One we played as kids."

My brows furrow, intrigue and excitement mixing in with the other emotions wrangling my nerves tight. "What game?"

For a second, I'm not sure if he hears my hushed question through the crowd of patrons, but then he blows out a low chuckle. "A simple game of hide and seek. If I find you, I get something."

This makes me turn, my eyes quickly taking in his features to gauge his seriousness. When he lifts a brow and casually picks up his drink, I decide to entertain him. "And what would you get?"

He takes a long swig from his glass, his Adam's apple bobbing as he swallows hard. "A secret of yours."

"We tell each other everything already," I counter, ignoring the surge of my pulse.

Adrian shakes his head, the cup clinking against the bar as he sets it down. "No, Bambi. I don't think we do."

His implication is more than obvious, and suddenly, I'm not as nervous as I once was. Things have always been murky when it comes to our relationship. The whole thing constantly teetering on the precipice of something more.

It's as though we've been standing at the edge of the pool. Both of us see the beauty and possibility of what it'd be like to take a swim, but also the terrifying notion of what will happen if we don't know how to swim.

What he's proposing feels like plunging into the deep end, forcing us to sink or swim. But I guess we already passed dipping our toes when I stayed in the bathroom.

Without giving myself time to reconsider, I grab his drink and down it in four lucky gulps. The earthy flavor soothes my frayed nerves, giving me the little bit of courage I need. "Okay."

Adrian runs his tongue over one of his canines, making my mouth dry up instantly. "Okay, what? I need to hear you agree to the terms. *Explicitly*."

My eyes widen a fraction before taking a quick inventory of the surrounding guests. Everyone is engrossed in their own conversations, clearly unattuned to the fact I'm about to agree to a game of hide and seek in exchange for a confession I'm not entirely sure I'm ready to give. While my sister has kept herself at the end of the bar, the same smug smirk is still painting her face.

I shift back to him and take a breath, though it sounds more like a heady sigh. "I agree to the game. If you win, I'll give you a secret. And if I win, I want one."

His brows lift and his lips pull down in surprise. "How will we determine who wins?"

I catch my lip between my teeth and ponder for a second. "If you find me in under ten minutes, you win. Ten minutes, one second, I win."

Adrian grins before nodding. "Okay."

I guffaw. "I need to hear it, *explicitly*."

A nerve in his jaw tics as his smile grows. "If I can't find you in under ten minutes, I'll give you a secret."

He holds out a hand. My shoulders shake with my laughter, as I oblige and take his hand in mine. It's something about the seriousness of a children's game with conditions being sealed with a handshake that has me relaxing.

But when I try to release his hand, he pulls me close, our chests an inch apart as he returns his face to my ear. I swallow hard around the surge of my pulse and hold my breath when he whispers, "Once I find you, there's no going back. It will change *everything*. So I advise you to choose your spot wisely, Bambi."

He releases me as quickly as he drew me in, before slipping his phone from his pocket. "Hey, Siri. Set me a timer for ten minutes."

Hide & Seek

CHAPTER NINE

Samantha

T he little robotic voice from his phone lets me know my time has begun, prompting me to get my ass out of the chair. Slowly, I slip off the stool, my skin tingling from Adrian's lingering gaze.

Excitement blooms through my core, and just like that, my adrenaline is coursing. The rushing of my blood is the only thing I can hear as I take my first step toward the exit. It's as though something long forgotten has clicked, setting me on edge and urging my feet to move.

I don't even bother looking back at Adrian or my sister, but instead, train my eyes forward. My pulse beats in time with the sudden countdown in my head, letting me know a rough estimate of how much time is left. Meanwhile, the eagerness flushing through my veins makes me hyper-aware of my surroundings.

I weave through the crowd, noting the number of people Adrian will have to move between in order to reach the doors.

It will be harder for him considering his size, so I have a buffer to add to my time.

Within a minute, I'm back in the lobby. It's beginning to fill with guests, but with our check-in system, the counter isn't overwhelmed. The chatter of nearby conversations drowns out as my ears perk up for anything that sounds even remotely close to Adrian.

His walk is telling—muted, yet heavy. It's how he's always managed to get me out of my good spots when we were kids. I'd think he'd given up and would come out, and *bam*, he'd be there waiting to tackle me to the ground and tickle me till I screamed uncle. It took a few times before I figured out how to listen for the floors to creak beneath his weight. Or the squish of a mat under his boot. Even the wood whined as he climbed the steps.

But now, something tells me none of that will help. If he does catch me, I won't be tickled, and uncle won't stop him.

Through the cluster of the other guests, I manage to slip past the receptionist without her noticing. Nor does the busy bellboy, who is loading up two carts of overnight bags.

Down the hall, I open the large wooden doors. I knew from the moment he said to hide, where I'd go. Maybe it's because deep down I know this will be one of the first places he looks. Which probably means I want to tell him my secret. I want him to know how I feel. How I've felt since I realized my love ran deeper than the heart.

But I also have a plan to get something out of him too. Because before I say anything, I need to know—really know—what exactly it is he feels when *he* looks at *me*.

I'm ready to play as many games as he wants, but guessing won't be one.

Inside the room, I lift the heavy curtains and squeeze

inside, repositioning the fabric so it falls naturally over my frame.

When I'm satisfied and nearly out of breath, I wait.

Adrian

She's hiding. Samantha is fucking *hiding*.

I'm lucky enough to have her in my life, not only as a supporter, but a friend. My best friend. To think for one minute that she may be into something so fundamentally important to me is... unreal.

My entire chest vibrates as I check the time on my phone. It's only been two minutes since she took off, but the anticipation—the *pull*—is killing me. It's a deep-seated hunger that will only be satisfied when the prey is in my hands. When her body is beneath mine, submissive and writhing with want.

She will be my greatest hunt yet, and if I have it my way, she'll be my last.

I set my empty glass back down and nod to Willow, who has been conveniently tied up until her sister disappeared in the crowd. She floats to my end of the bar and grabs the empty cup, slipping it beneath her in the bin.

"I should have guessed primal a long time ago. It makes so much sense now," she says, wiping off the counter with the smuggest of smirks on her face. "That was your favorite game when we were younger."

Considering her box of treasures I stumbled upon a few years ago, it doesn't surprise me in the slightest she knows what a primal kink is. "That it was. Who would have known it would turn into something like this."

"Oh, believe me, I see the appeal." Willow leans over, examining me with her amber eyes.

At first, I mirror her grin and tilt my head, but then an idea strikes. Willow is the only one who knows the small part of Sam I don't, and while yes, I want Bambi to be the one to tell me, I can't lie about the slight ache resonating in the back of my heart. The sliver of doubt still holding on tight. "You think she'll go for it?"

This makes Willow throw her head back with laughter, garnering a few stray looks from some of the patrons. "For you? Absolutely. You have no idea, Stokes."

Hope flares in my chest with her unsaid confirmation, snuffing out some of the uncertainty. My eyes flash to the clock.

Five minutes.

Plenty of time, considering I only need one.

The forewarning I gave her was not meant to be a deterrent, but a test of a few things. One, if she'd actually accept the terms of the game. Two, if she trusts me enough to do something like hiding in a hotel with no real idea of what will happen when I find her.

Lastly, if she goes to the only place I intend to look, she wants this as badly as I do.

And I plan to reward her accordingly.

I hand my debit card to Will. "Guess I'll find out soon."

You'd think hiding in a mass of thick velvet curtains, counting to sixty, nine times over, would be calming to the heart. Perhaps even give me time to think things over and contemplate how wrong I may be that he'd come here first.

But it doesn't. I know Adrian. I know any second, he'll walk through the door, and snatch me up, and... well, I'm not sure what's going to happen, but I know it will change everything. As he implied, we're already past a point of return.

We're jumping in the pool and all I can do now is hope like hell we both know how to swim.

My heart has also not returned to normal. If anything, the sheer anticipation is keeping it at a calorie-burning rate. One minute left.

I force myself to suck in a slow ten-second breath, then push it out. I do this twice before it happens. The sound.

The sway of one door opening, then the snap of it closing, followed by the clunk of the lock.

He's here.

And he knows I am too.

My body begins to quiver, my throat turns dry, and the air is no longer filling my lungs. This is it.

The sound of his boots meeting the carpet is nothing more than a muffled shuffle, but the sound is incredibly nerve-wracking. They're slow and paced out. Purposeful. But he isn't getting closer. No, he's nearing the–

As soon as I think it, a b-flat minor chord echoes throughout the ballroom. The sound winds around my spine, and my eyes squeeze shut.

"I found you, Bambi." Adrian's voice is much deeper than normal, almost a husky growl that forces my thighs to squeeze together. "I want my prize."

I lift my hand slowly and clamp it over my mouth. He may know I'm in here, but not where, and I have at least twenty seconds left–more than enough time to win.

The sudden strike of the piano makes me jolt, and his

chuckle is immediate. "There you are. Be a good sport and come out. I mean, unless you prefer I come get you."

Flustered, I allow myself another minute before beginning to draw the curtains from around me. The heavy fabric is somehow harder to move, but as I begin fighting with the damn things, they suddenly open, Adrian slipping inside with me.

A small squeak falls from my lips, making him laugh again. "Did I scare you?"

I shake my head, attempting to regain some type of control of my body, which is currently going haywire. "No, just startled. I didn't hear you."

He jerks the curtain open, untangling me while also encasing us in a small sort of bubble. When he takes a step toward me, I bite into my lip, a heaviness sinking low in my stomach. I'm positive he notices, but instead of calling attention to it, he lifts his phone, showing me the screen.

Four.

Three.

Two.

One.

"Now, for my secret." He smiles, silencing the alarm and slipping the phone back into his front pocket. "I want to know what my name sounds like when you come."

Adrian

Samantha's eyes widen as she processes what I said—which, in her defense, was *not* what I originally planned to ask. It just... came out. "I mean, it's only fair, considering you know what your name sounds like."

She clears her throat, blinking a few times before steeling her voice. "Are you sure that's what you want to use your win for?"

My brows furrow, my head jerking back slightly. Now it's my turn to be surprised. "I'd say that's the best prize."

Her light pink tongue slips out, wetting her lips. I want to lean down and suck it into my mouth, see if I can taste the croissant still lingering on her taste buds. Or maybe the drink she decided to steal from me at the bar. She shifts her weight from heel to heel before deciding on something and closing her eyes.

Confused, I wait, curiosity forcing me to watch as both her hands come up on either side of her and fist the thick velvet surrounding her head.

In the next second, her chest starts heaving up and down, a rose color blooming over her cheeks. By the time I realize what she's doing, it's too late for me to redact my request.

"*Adrian.*"

Fucking hell.

I don't know what I thought it would sound like, but whatever I could have imagined doesn't hold a candle to her molted moan. It's breathy and desperate, a plea coating every syllable. It's pure and unfiltered want, surging the blood straight to my already stiff cock.

I move quickly, pressing a hand over her mouth and closing what little space is between us. "That will do, Bambi."

She peels her eyes open far too slowly, a smug smile lifting my hand. Her gaze roves over my face, then down to my fingers, which I remove. She drops her arms.

"Is it what you expected?"

"No," I answer honestly.

"It sounds better when I'm actually coming." Her lashes

57

flutter when she realizes what she's revealed, but I don't give her the chance to paddle backward.

"How often?"

Sam's face falls and I hook my forefinger under her chin and bring her eyes back to mine. "Don't do that. You've never hidden from me before. Don't start now."

She gives me a curt nod, but instead of releasing her face, I move to the right, running my thumb along her jaw. She leans into my touch, and it's then I decide I can't wait.

If she learns about my needs and decides it's too much, I'll be able to handle it because I've had her. Even if it's just this.

"I'm going to kiss you now, Bambi. Is that okay?"

She nods again, but when I don't immediately move, she whispers a quick, "Yes."

Quick learner.

Just as I've imagined every time I close my eyes, her lips fit mine perfectly. They were made to cushion my hard blows, to open to my demanding tongue, to cradle my need for dominance.

I pin my body to hers, threading my fingers through her brown strands and drawing us closer. She moans into my mouth, grinding her body against mine as she wraps her arms around my head.

We stay like this until we both can't breathe, giving, taking, and fighting to get closer than we already are. When I finally rip my mouth from hers, I tighten my grip on one side of her head, forcing it to lull to the side as I graze my teeth down her neck.

She shudders against me, and it takes more self-control than I thought possible not to bite her neck and say fuck everything else. Luckily, it seems Sam's own curiosity is begging to be answered.

"I want a rematch."

"Come again?" I ask against the column of her throat, my nose trailing up and down her soft skin.

She moves a hand to my chest and presses so lightly it almost feels like just a touch, but I know better. I've committed myself to learn signs of nervousness and withdrawing consent without a clear verbal indicator.

I take a small step back, releasing her while granting her enough space so she feels safe, but not rejected in any way.

She clears her throat and lowers her hands to the waistband of my jeans. Her gaze stays trained there as she brushes her finger softly over the denim. "I want a rematch. I have questions I'd like answered."

"You don't need a rematch to ask. I'll answer whatever you'd like to know."

She shakes her head but still doesn't look up. "No. I want to play."

"Play what?" I hook my finger under her chin again until she peers up at me from behind her fan of dark lashes. Her innocent eyes are on full display, and the mere image sends my dick straining against its confines.

"I want to play tag."

CHAPTER TEN

Adrian kissed me. Really kissed me.

And it wasn't only the fact his kiss brought me to the edge of the world, shown the vast universe, then plunged back into gravity. It was how *right* it felt. Utterly and indisputably right.

I think after being friends with someone for so long, ruining a good friendship isn't the only concern that arises. It's also the fear of no spark. Of realizing you wasted a certain amount of time waiting and wanting and wishing, only to be let down.

But what just happened makes me angry with myself that I didn't do anything sooner. In fact, I want to spend the rest of my night doing nothing but drowning in his kiss, but there's something I want more.

His truth. The entire thing. And in order to get it, I want to continue this game of cat and mouse. Why?

Because whatever we did, was fun. It was exhilarating and childish, but sexy and terrifying. It made me feel alive, and why not lessen the strain of the heavy questions we'll ask with a game of tag?

"So, let me make sure I understand you correctly, Sam." Adrian rolls up his sleeves, exposing the strong arms that were holding me in place just moments ago. "You want to run

outside? Through the crowd of paraders, down the back alleys, and into the wooded park of Boston Common."

I push the curtain back into place as we move from behind it and into the ballroom. "You did a very good job of repeating me word for word."

He rolls his eyes, but I hear the genuine seriousness in his words. "I'm big on complete and total understanding."

"Ah, being explicit. I gathered as much."

Adrian sits down at the edge of the piano bench, leaning his forearms against his knees. "Full comprehension and consent are important, Bambi. As are safewords."

Safewords. Now, I'm not inept, so I know safewords generally involve things that could get out of hand, but never have I been with someone who needed them.

"Something tells me he likes more adventurous things than a little self-exploration."

Willow's words replay in my mind, the connection suddenly becoming glaringly obvious. My steadily thumping heart is the only audible thing in the room as we stare at one another, understanding settling between us.

"So I'll need a safeword?"

Adrian stands and catches my fingertips in his hands. He doesn't pull me closer but keeps us connected, his eyes softening as he searches my face. "Yes. Is that something you're comfortable with?"

I try to nod, swallowing around the lump lodged in my throat. He gives me a soft smile, and I realize what he wants. "Yes, I am."

He takes a small step closer, forcing me to lift my chin to keep our gazes connected. "I need you to know something, Bambi. I've waited a long time for this. I won't be sweet, soft, or anything remotely close to gentle. This will be years of pent-up desire, unleashed in a way that will leave you a fucking *mess*. Are you sure this is what you want?"

His admission stops my breath. It slows time and splits my heart in two. Everything aches and feels so terribly good at the same time, my body can barely form the necessary speech to tell him how badly I've wanted him to say that, how long I've waited to hear it.

Somehow, I push it out. It's an almost inaudible whisper, but my conviction is impossible to miss. "Yes."

A delicious smirk stretches across his face, lighting up my insides all over again. He presses a soft kiss on my nose. "Good. Are you ready to play your game of tag?"

"We don't have to if you..." I trail off, with the knowledge of everything wedging in between us, making me realize the important questions I had before have already been answered.

"Oh no, Bambi. We're playing this game. And it won't be the only one."

My pussy clenches around nothing, and the low-bearing ache starts up all over again. Why am I so turned on by the thought of him chasing me? And not only that, but the need to have a word to keep me safe?

All our lives, I've only ever known Adrian to be a gentle giant. He's big, brawny, and scary as hell, with a sharp jaw and hooded eyes. On the field, he's even worse—a total animal, really. But with me, he's simply Adrian. Expert foot massager, wonderful at picking random monster movies that actually end up being good, and popcorn throw-it-across-the-couch-and-into-your-mouth extraordinaire. He's kind, compassionate, and refuses to use single-use plastics.

Don't get me wrong, I'm tired of slow and sweet. I want something to take my breath away. I want him to devour me whole and leave me curled up like a dead little spider. But to picture him as anything other than what I've known is impossible.

Still, I'm dying to find out. "Uncle."

His brows snap together. "What?"

A vicious blush takes over my face. "The, um, safeword. If it's dumb–"

"No." He presses a kiss to my forehead, making me melt. "It's perfect."

Something about him approving my word choice makes my heart flutter. Like I've read his mind and plucked it from his head. I like that.

"Be safe, Sam. Don't trip and fall, or run into anyone. Don't be so caught up looking for me that you aren't paying attention." He drops my hand as he gives me the pregame speech, as if this was his idea. "The point is to have fun, and not get hurt. Not until I find you, at least."

My nerves prickle. "You plan to hurt me."

He nods once. "In the best ways. And not more than you can handle."

A tremor runs through my spine at his promise. At the possibilities of what he could mean. "Okay."

"I'll count to thirty, Bambi. Then I'm coming for you."

The nighttime crowd is much thicker than I anticipated. Hues of bright colors mix as I make a pitiful attempt to maneuver around them on the congested sidewalk.

The parade is in full effect. Rows of men in kilts blowing into heavy bagpipes move down the center of the road. They're led by a red-haired leprechaun wielding a staff of sorts in one hand and a water gun in the other. He's dancing around in front of them, hyping the spectators up while women twirl around him, tossing out beads and glowing necklaces.

I squeeze inside the group, my thirty-second head start now a mere ten as I push through. The noise of the crowd grows louder, shrieks of sheer giddiness filling the air. Suddenly, a cluster of people right in front of me part, avoiding a woman who's getting doused in some type of glowing paint shooting out of the leprechaun's squirt gun.

Three. I veer to the right, then circle the people behind her.

Two. Just a few more feet and I can turn down the alley.

One. My heart flutters.

He's coming.

With a few hushed "excuse mes" and another round of narrowly missed paint, I make it to the alley. It's a free shot to the woods, which backs into the entire strip of businesses. My feet pick up pace, adrenaline whooshing through my system, giving me the false confidence I'll actually make it.

I only move about five yards.

A smaller back street opens up behind the tire shop I passed, and Adrian must have been waiting. He careens out of the dark and barrels into me, catching me around the waist and nearly throwing me against the wall of the business.

My ass hits the hard brick, sending a sharp bite of pain down my legs, but his arm protects my back from the same fate, squeezing me close to him.

His free arm is pressing into the wall on the other side of my head, effectively caging me in. Our matching heavy breaths mingle in the cool air, my breasts brushing against him with every intake of air. My nipples tingle, hardening under the feel of his hard chest as I examine his face.

His jaw is clenched tight, a nerve pulsing on the side, as his eyes rove over my face. "Are you hurt?"

I start to shake my head, but stop. "No."

He smiles. "Hmm. Good."

"How'd you catch me so quickly?" I internally curse how out of breath I sound.

"Did I spoil the fun?" he whispers, running his nose along the shell of my ear.

I shiver, my hands tingling at my sides to thread my fingers through his hair and pull him closer. "No."

"Well then, it seems I'm owed another secret."

"What do you want to know?" The words are barely audible above the crowd a few yards away. My eyes flash down the alley, with the realization that anyone who turns around would see how incredibly intimate we appear. But instead of deterring me, it excites me more, sending another wave of shivers down my arms.

"I want to know if I slip my fingers inside of you right now how drenched you would be."

The overwhelming need pulsing in my clit fuels me. "Find out."

Adrian jerks his head back and meets my gaze. He must see something in my eyes that tells him how serious I am, because he lets out a deep growl of approval. It rumbles through my chest and settles deep in my core.

He unhooks his hand from around my waist and lightly trails it around, lifting my shirt enough for his fingers to make tortuous contact. The entire time he moves, he never breaks eye contact, watching as my face undergoes the shifts from my increasing arousal. By the time he reaches the button of my jeans, I'm nearly panting.

"Let's see, shall we?"

I saw my bottom lip between my teeth as I nod. "Let's."

A delicious smirk curls one side of his mouth before he somehow pops my button in one swift move, then drags my zipper down so slowly I feel each click of the metal separating.

When his hand slips beneath the thin lace of my panties, I can't keep the moan from slipping out, or my eyes from squeezing shut.

"I need your eyes on me when I'm touching you, Bambi." His fingers dip dangerously low, the whisper of his touch against my clit causing me to hiss and my eyes to fly open.

Adrian smirks and slides the fabric to the side before gliding a finger from my entrance to my throbbing clit, the sensation causing a moan to get stuck in my throat. "Cocky little thing. You wanted me to see how wet you are. All for me."

A deep, involuntary rumble vibrates through my chest at the sound of his voice taunting me, matching the neediness of my strangled moan. My back arches on instinct while I tilt my hips into his palm. That one little swipe felt so damn good. "Again."

He leans forward, nipping my chin. "For another secret."

"Anything." I can't help my hips from searching for more friction, but his hand holds me still.

"Oh, Sam. Don't say that."

"Adrian." My voice is a borderline plea. "Ask me what you want to know."

He chuckles against my throat before withdrawing abruptly. My chest nearly caves, the loss of his touch tearing the seams of my fragile edges. Before I can make a smart remark, he holds his finger up between us.

My arousal coats the digit, the evidence shimmering in the low light of the alley. He presses his fingertip into his mouth and licks it clean. My stomach clenches as his eyes roll and he groans against the taste.

When he's done, I'm half delirious, my heart fluttering so

fast, I feel it everywhere. Finally, he drops his hand from the brick, buttoning my pants up.

I start to protest, but a gleam in Adrian's eye stops me. He steps forward, dipping his head, and his hands find my hips. His fingers dig into the soft flesh, his warm breath coasting along the column of my neck as he rumbles in my ear.

"I want to play again."

He takes a wide step back, allowing the cool air to sprout goosebumps down my arms.

"Now?" Still half dizzy from the moment, I almost forgot I was supposed to reach the woods.

But then he smirks, and every nerve I have tingles in unison all over again. "Go on, Bambi. Don't make it easy on me."

My pulse soars, my heart thumping against my rib cage as I watch him give me more space.

"This time I want to hunt you. I want to struggle to find you." He glances down at his finger and then back at me. "I'll give you a ten second head start."

I suck in a sharp breath; the idea of being not only chased, but hunted, making my skin hot all over. Adrian's smile fades, and a heavy realization settles in. He's serious, and when he catches me this time, I know *exactly* what's going to happen.

Finally, I take a step forward, halting in enough time to see his eyes lower, a hooded, predatory gaze taking over.

"Run."

The Hunt

CHAPTER ELEVEN

Samantha

The cool wind slaps against my face as I sprint through the alley. No matter how much adrenaline pumps through my veins, or how fast I think I'm moving, my ten seconds will likely be up before I reach the edge of the woods. I force the possibility from my mind. If I don't, I won't be able to focus or maneuver through the thick cluster of trees when I reach them.

Luckily, they're extremely close together on the outskirts of the park, one tree no more than a foot away from the next. They stretch high into the night sky, drowning out most light pollution. This plays in my favor, considering I'm in dark clothes and he has on another white Henley.

Unfortunately, though, because of the darkness, I will have a hard time winding through. I'll need to be careful not to fall, and even more so not to make a lot of noise while I'm running.

The count in my head reaches zero just as my hand makes contact with the first tree. The rough texture of the

bark scratches against my palm while I use it to guide me inside.

My heart hammers in my chest, my nerves nearly vibrating through me, but I push through, focusing on the excitement swirling in my stomach. I mean, I want him to catch me, but there's a part of me that's completely terrified of what exactly he's going to do.

I have an idea, though the idea of needing a safeword makes me anxious, but in a good, I'm-probably-going-to-pass-out-from-the-pleasure-way.

Dead leaves and twigs crunch under my shoes, but thinking about it, it's nearly impossible to be quiet until I get deeper inside, where the trees begin to thin out more.

A stray skinny branch nicks me in the shoulder, and I have to cover my mouth to keep the curse from spewing out. I'm already making more than enough noise, since the bagpipes and cheers are fading the farther I go.

I take a few turns, my body instinctively leading me to the spot we all used to visit when we were younger. There's a clearing not too far ahead that has trees with low, but strong branches I can climb.

An image of Adrian yanking me from a tree invades my mind. He said he planned to hurt me, and though I'm not one hundred percent sure how, I wonder if he's rough enough to do that. If he plans to command everything that's coming.

Is the Adrian in bed the same tender, loving man I've known nearly my whole life? Or is he rough and rugged, ready to leave marks and bruises of his victory?

I pull in a hard breath, my pussy quivering from the thought. I've dreamt of excitement for so long, and how I thought spanking or a throat grab would suffice, I'll never know.

Finally, I break through a tight cluster of trees and into the clearing. Just as I remember when we played here as kids, there's a large stump in the center, surrounded by a patch of deep green clovers. Overhead, the once clear sky is now painted in dark clouds, hiding the stars.

I rush across the clearing and reach for one of the low-bearing branches. But when I hoist myself up and bear my weight down on it, it snaps, coming with me when my back hits the forest floor.

This time I can't hold back the groan escaping my lips as a spike of pain shoots up my spine. "Damn it."

I roll to the side at the same time a heavy snap echoes in the air.

Adrian

It takes everything in me to give her the full ten seconds as I watch her flee down the alley, her long brown strands whipping behind her.

After feeling her, *tasting* her, the beast in my chest is hungry, eager for the chase, and the short run to find her in the alley isn't enough to satiate him.

He needs more. So much more.

Pure adrenaline pumps through my veins as I count down, my arms shaking at my sides as I bounce from one foot to the next. When I reach five, I bend down and ensure my boots are tied.

By the time I stand, her time is up.

The crowd and music fade into the background. The lights from the parade dim to darkness. The brick walls shift into tall tree trunks. My feet carry me faster than I've ever moved before.

The entrance to the woods is tight, but I rip through, ignoring the bites of pain from stray branches catching on my sleeve. I push them up my forearms as I veer to the left, the hunger growing stronger the closer I get to the spot I know she's headed.

Five yards. Even if it wasn't for the fact she's cracking branches beneath her feet, I can smell her scent trailing behind her. Once I tasted the sweet musk of her cunt, I became addicted. Savored and memorized what I'll soon get to claim.

Four yards. She's in front of me now, tearing through the trees as fast as she can, her breath coming out in pants that match the steady beat of my heart. I love that she doesn't hear me. I'll have to teach her how to be quieter when she's running from me.

Three yards. She makes a swift turn to the left, disappearing behind a group of trees almost too close for me to follow behind. When I reach it and realize I can't, my beast roars, lust and desire surging through me, spurring me on.

My heart barrels into my rib cage as I pick up the pace, doubling back until I find a way in at the same time I hear her groaning.

Sam rolls to her stomach as I break through the trees. She jumps to her feet, positioning herself, as if ready to take off at any second.

I like that she thinks she can outrun me. That I won't scour the fucking earth to find her.

We stare at each other from across the opening for two seconds, both of us clearly deciding what to do next. There's nothing between us but the thick stump and cool breeze.

As if on cue, a heavy rumble of thunder sounds overhead, prompting us to move.

I race across, eating the space between us in seconds, while she turns and attempts to climb up the tree she must have fallen from.

For a moment, I consider seeing if she can manage the feat, but my beast decides not to let her get away.

I'm done playing with my meal.

Samantha

Adrian catches me around the waist and yanks me down. He flips us around and has my back pinned to the tree before I take my next breath.

Different from the alley, where he merely caged me in, he captures both my wrists in one of his big hands and holds them steady above my head, effectively holding me in place. The rough texture of the wood pinches my skin, but somehow the small bites of pain don't bother me. In fact, it enhances the arousal slinking through me.

"I found you, Bambi," he growls, his eyes burning into me. "And I keep what I catch."

"Like finders keepers?" I breathe, my heart singing from what his words imply.

Though his gaze remains deadly, his lips twitch, a hint of a grin playing at the edges. "Yes. You're mine now, Samantha."

I don't get the chance to respond to him, nor the euphoria filling me to the brim before he captures my lips.

Unlike our first kiss, this one is wild. It's hungry and intense and Adrian completely devours me. His free hand snakes under my shirt and dips into my bra, his fingers finding and pinching my pebbled nipple.

I arch into him, moaning into his mouth as the pain melts into pleasure, prompting him to do it again to the other one, only harder. A whimper escapes, the need growing so strong I feel on the verge of tears.

He releases my mouth with an angry groan, removing his hand from my shirt and grabbing my chin to look at him. "You remember the safeword?"

"Yes."

"And you understand I plan to brand you in every way possible? From my mouth to my cock, you will bear all of me."

My entire body squeezes, the promises of him and a possibility of us, doing all the right things to my libido. "Yes, Adrian. I want to wake up feeling you everywhere."

His pupils flare. "And you will. That I can promise."

He yanks the hem of my shirt, and in one fluid motion, he rips it from my body. I squeak at the feel of the fabric snapping against my skin, but before I realize what's happening, he binds my hands together with the ripped shirt.

The chilly breeze does little to cool the fire raging across my exposed flesh. Instead, only intensifies the dozens of sensations skirting across it.

He jerks me away from the tree before picking me up and hurling me over his shoulder as though I weigh nothing. My heart leaps into my throat, causing my squeal of surprise to sound more like a garbled gasp.

Adrian chuckles as he turns, walking to the center of the clearing and stopping in front of the massive tree stump. He latches his fingers on the waistband of my jeans while the other hand presses into the middle of my back.

I know what he's going to do, but the whoosh from the

wind in my ears as he tosses me on the stump still makes my stomach flip.

My body lays in the direct center, my head a foot from the edge while my knees hang off the other end. He towers over me, his dark gaze lighting a path down my body. I physically feel it when his eyes linger on a spot too long. It's as though he's committing me to memory; every dip, freckle, and curve.

I love it. I love that there's no part of me that feels self-conscious, or nervous of his inspection. He's my best friend. He's seen me at my absolute worst and still told me I was beautiful. Still made me *feel* beautiful. It's one of the many things he's done to make me love him.

Adrian leans forward, pressing a kiss to my forehead as though he heard my thoughts. It causes the butterflies to take flight, the small moment of affection slicing through everything else and making me melt.

"You have no idea how long I've waited for this," he whispers, running a hand down my waist.

"Not as long as me."

His eyes flash to me, a storm raging in the irises. "Biggest mistake of my life was not kissing you that day."

My eyes close, a burn radiating across the brim while my heart pinches, but he doesn't let me sit with the ache. Instead, he lifts my hands above my head and digs in his pocket for a switchblade.

He flips it open and stabs it through the center of the fabric, locking me in place. My chest heaves up and down as I watch him move down the rest of my body. Within a minute, my bra, jeans, and lace panties are thrown to the floor, disappearing in a thick patch of clovers.

Fully at his mercy, and exposed completely, Adrian's gaze takes on a hungry one. He returns to my mouth, kissing me greedily. I arch into him, lust expanding and forcing everything else to the wayside as I feel his erection through his jeans.

He lets my lips go, trailing his down my neck. He sucks in bits of skin on his way, nipping and biting with varying force. I yelp and moan, shift and writhe, the wood beneath me creating a rough type of friction. The pain and pleasure combine, covering my vision with stars from the delirium.

He sucks one of my nipples into his mouth, swirling his tongue before clamping down on the soft flesh.

"Adrian!" I scream, my body quivering from need. "Please."

He ignores my whimpers and moves down, his teeth grazing over my hip and to one side of my thigh. "You're so fucking gorgeous, and I..." he trails off, falling to his knees. "Am fucking *starving*."

Adrian

In one rough motion, I spread her legs wide open. Her cries of need fuel me on as I press my face between her thighs and take an insatiable inhale.

She smells so damn good. Like her scent was made for me to hunt. *To find. To own.* My cock somehow hardens further at the thought, pressing painfully into my jeans.

Unable to withstand another minute not tasting her, I lick her from entrance to clit, a deep groan rumbling my chest as she coats my tongue. She's soaked. Her pussy is covered in her want, and trembling with need.

My beast longs to be released from his cage, but in fear of

doing too much, too soon, I continue to keep a steady pace. It isn't soft and tentative, but also isn't all teeth and tight holds.

She tries to close her legs around my head, but I grab her thighs, spreading her more, as I continue to fuck her with my tongue. It doesn't take long before she's teetering on the edge, her nerves already so worked up from her first run, she's in need of release.

One of my hands disappears from her thigh, and my finger plunges into her warm cunt. She moans at the intrusion, her back arching off the stump as she presses herself closer to my face.

"Needy little prey, aren't you?" I chuckle against her clit before sucking it into my mouth.

This time, she yelps, the bite of pain being exactly what she needed. Her walls begin fluttering, gripping my fingers with her impending orgasm. And it's then I decide.

I make a promise to myself to take my time with her later, to worship her how she deserves. But for now, I want to completely devour her, imprint myself on every inch of her beautiful skin, and own every orgasm she ever has.

Yanking myself from her body, I grab her by the waist. A despairing little whimper escapes her as I carefully, but quickly, flip her over, turning it into a gasp, and watch as the blade tilts when the fabric twists with the move.

My hands grab onto her hips, hard, forcing her to pull her knees up on the stump, which puts her ass in the perfect position.

The deep primal satisfaction at seeing her like this takes over, and the urge to breech that tight ring of muscle is almost overbearing as I shove my fingers back into her shining pussy. I fuck her with my digits until she's back on the edge, her body nearly convulsing around me.

"Come for me, love," I command, twisting my finger to hit her G-spot.

"*Adrian!*" When she cries out my name, I begin circling her clit with my thumb while bending to bite into the soft flesh of her ass, sending her tumbling into the abyss. Her walls grip onto my fingers in the waves of her orgasm, while my free hands work quickly to unbuckle my pants and free my throbbing erection. I stroke myself as I let her ride it out, but when the last clench of her pussy is weak, I line the head up to her entrance and slip my fingers out.

"Alright, Sam. Play time's over," I tell her just before I slam inside.

Samantha

CHAPTER TWELVE

I saw how big Adrian was while watching him in the shower. I thought because I was aware, I could anticipate how he'd feel. But *nothing,* not even my orgasm still dripping down my thighs, could have helped me accommodate his size when he drives into me.

I suck in a sharp breath, my toes curling as he slides out and plunges back in. My nails nearly break from gripping into the stump as he stretches me, filling me to the hilt. He does this again and again, wild groans and strangled breaths pouring into the air around us, accompanied by my stifled whimpers.

It's euphoria and agony rolled into one–an indescribable pain that dissolves as quickly as it comes, transforming into blinding pleasure.

"Do you hear that? You're so fucking wet, Sam. So fucking perfect."

I actually mewl at his words, emotions expanding in my chest and heightening my awareness to everywhere he's connected to me. His touch is both burning and soothing, creating a conundrum of sensations I can't pick out individually.

He moves faster, his cock dragging through me before hitting a spot that took years of self-exploration to find. It's as

though he knows me better than I know myself, and it makes me hate that we waited so long to finally do this.

To give in.

"How are you doing that?" I cry out, loving the feel of his fingers digging into my hips.

He won't let me move. I'm completely at his mercy–stuck–only able to receive what he's willing to give me. And he's giving me everything I can take.

A clap of thunder rolls overhead, matching the growls Adrian releases every time he plows back inside of me. He feels too good, too perfect. I bite my hand, the overwhelming sensation bubbling to the surface, while the threat of my face being so close to the knife ignites a different type of excitement altogether. The polished silver acts as a mirror, allowing me to watch as he moves in and out, while his mouth forms a near animalistic snarl.

I bite harder, muffling my desperate whines.

One of Adrian's hands snakes around and palms my breast, his finger pinching my pebbled nipple, making me gasp. "Don't do that. I want to hear you. I want everyone to hear how I make you feel."

His hand disappears from my nipple and moves up, wrapping around the blade before yanking it from the stump and using it to cut through the makeshift bondage. He pulls himself out of me, before hauling my body from the wood and tossing me on my back in the patch of clovers.

My hair fans out amongst the plants, a heavy contrast against the dark greenery. Adrian must think so too, because the same predatory gaze from earlier is back. A nerve in his jaw tics and his eyes lower, becoming almost scary.

But God, do I love it.

My instinct should be to move, to try and run, but he must

see it cross my features because he lifts both my legs above his shoulders and slams back inside of me.

I gasp, the position allowing him to hit much deeper spots, decorating my vision with little white stars. His iron grip holds me in place as his head moves to the side. He grazes his teeth along one of my calves before slipping off both my shoes I hadn't even realized were still on. When he reaches the arch in my foot, he nips the tight flesh, chuckling when I hiss through my teeth.

Adrian caresses the spot with his thumb, kneading it lightly. "I'm the only one who gets to massage these feet. Understand."

His gravelly voice makes my insides flutter. "Yes."

"That's my girl."

He starts his pace slowly, tilting my hips to give me the perfect view of his cock sliding out of me, glimmering in my wetness.

"*Adrian*," I whimper.

"Say it," he growls, knowing exactly what I want. What I've already become addicted to.

I swallow around the pulse thrumming in my throat. "Harder."

He smirks, parting his mouth to lick over the top row of his teeth. "My needy, needy prey."

Then, he fucks me. His fingers dig into the flesh of my hips, holding tight as he rams into me with abandon. He completely loses himself, fucking me relentlessly while a mix of groans and growled curses falls from his lips.

I scrape my nails down his arm in an attempt to gather any type of leverage. But when he hisses at the sharp contact, I fall in love with the sound and jab my nails in deeper.

A fire builds low in my belly, the constant friction of him dragging along my spot, pushing me closer to another orgasm.

Adrian must notice the change and drops my legs, leaning

forward to capture my lips. The kiss is hungry, his tongue tangling with mine before licking every corner of my mouth. It's filled with words we can't say, and new emotions I've never felt. By the time we come up for air, tremors are running through my spine, a new knowledge somehow in place.

Neither of us addresses it, and instead, he lowers his hand, finding my throbbing clit with his thumb. He works it in hard circles, moving feverishly as his pace increases.

My head begins to swim, the budding pressure growing tight before finally exploding, erupting through my veins like fire. I scream out as the orgasm rips through me, grabbing Adrian's muscled back as he chases his own release, driving into me at a punishing pace. His head dips as he bites the space under my collarbone, a tremor working down his spine.

He comes as the sky splits open, his roar in tune with the rolls of thunder. Even as the soft rain pelts into his back, he continues to fuck me through his orgasm, a mix of his sweat and the water dripping onto my chest.

Our heavy breaths mingle in the air, the steady sprinkle of rain cooling my skin as we both come down from the high, neither of us too eager to move yet.

Adrian strokes my cheek with his thumb, his hazel eyes searching mine. When he finds what he's looking for, he smiles.

It seems too quick when he pulls from my body, but the sting of his loss fades when he lifts me from the forest floor and onto his lap. My heart flutters when he strokes my matted hair, tucking it behind my ear as he gazes down at my face.

I'm completely and utterly smitten, and have been for years. But something in this moment makes me realize I had no idea what really lay beneath the surface of what we could be. What we were always meant to be.

Adrian leans forward, pressing a soft kiss to my temple.

The rain has already slowed to a sprinkle, but small beads of it drip from his thick lashes. "Are you hurt?"

My head lulls, falling onto his shoulder. "Yes. But in the best ways."

He smirks, dropping his hand from my face and tracing over the bite marks he left behind. I tremble as he works his way down.

"I meant what I said, Sam." His voice is barely above a whisper, but I hear the slight nervousness in his words.

"You've said a lot of things today. Which one?" I hold my breath as I wait for his response, my delicate heart waiting for the one thing it's always wanted to hear. Granted, tonight has told me everything I need to know, but I still want him to say it.

"This changes everything." He swallows hard. "You are mine, and I am yours."

The warmth blooms in my chest before expanding outward, making me feel as if I'm floating. To know this is real, after all this time... I kiss him and smile.

"About damn time."

CHAPTER THIRTEEN

I t takes a bit of convincing, but I'm able to coerce Sam into wearing my shirt as we sneak in the back of the hotel. She's not a fan of the few glances I get being half-dressed, but my constant hold on her body seems to help while we head to the spare room.

Inside, I run us a shower and make quick work of undressing us both. She's sore. I can tell by the way she walks, the way her face scrunches together as I touch some of the more tender areas.

My beast is proud, her marks nothing more than evidence of a job well done. Though the softness in me, the best friend, is slightly more concerned.

"Are you sure you're okay?" I guide her into the shower, ignoring her huffs of annoyance.

"Yes, Adrian. I'm... perfect. Currently drowning in bliss. So don't ruin it with your hovering."

This makes me laugh. I hadn't planned to be so rough. I wanted to start slow, only wanted her to experience the chase. But I'm sort of glad she got to see a bit of both. See who I am.

This woman has my entire heart, has for longer than I'll admit, but for her to enjoy it the way she is... I don't think anything could make me feel more elated.

She hisses when the warm water meets her back, but then her eyes roll, and my shoulders relax. "God, this feels good. Get in here."

I smile and climb inside with her. "I need to wash you."

Her brows furrow. "I can wash myself, Adrian. I'm sore, but I'm not an igit."

I growl, shaking my head. "You're not an igit, but I have to do it."

"Why?"

There's a real curiosity in her question, and I decide now is as good a time as any to explain to her more in-depth what she's getting into. "Are you familiar with BDSM?"

Her beautiful brown eyes widen, and she nods.

I grab the loofah hanging from the shower caddy and jerk my head toward the body wash behind her. When she turns to grab it, my gaze follows her golden curves, noting every little fleck of dirt to the tiny pink crescents from my nails and teeth. It spikes my blood pressure, the need to be inside her growing all over again.

She swivels back and hands it to me. "So what we did in the woods... is it like your version of a red room?"

I bark out laughter as I pour soap onto the sponge. "Yes. Exactly that. I'm what people refer to as a primal Dom, and what we did was primal play."

"So we'll always end up this messy." She huffs, smiling as I create big suds. "Is that why you feel the need to clean me?"

"First, no. Taking care of you after we're a mess is something I *want* to do." I rub a soapy hand across her check, my heart warming when she leans into my touch. "But the technical term is called aftercare. Second, it doesn't always need to take place in the woods."

She pouts, and I don't think I've ever seen anything more adorable. "But that was fun and exciting."

Now, my tender heart swells in my chest. "So is hunting you through the hotel and fucking you in the alley."

Sam lets out a whimper, her lashes fluttering as though she's picturing it. I begin to wash her body, careful not to press too hard when I go over the more bruised spots. "It's different for everyone, but for me, primal play is a state of mind. My beast, or need to engage in primal activities, is triggered by different things. In our case, it's always been your smell."

Her head jolts back as she listens, but then almost immediately a lightbulb goes off in her head. "Stinky Sam."

I smirk and nod. "Stinky Sam wasn't because you stunk. It was because you smelled so fucking good, I wanted to bite you. I didn't understand why, and it freaked me out a bit. Made me worry you would think I was out of my mind."

"And is that the same reason we stopped wrestling and playing around?"

On a bent knee, I wash one of her feet before gazing back up at her. "Yes. We would get rough, and I would suddenly want to get rougher. I wanted to pin you down and make you submit. We were teens when I finally figured out I was actually aroused by it."

She tilts my chin up with her forefinger, prompting me to stand. "Why didn't you tell me?"

"Because I love you too much to lose you." The admission is both a heavy weight from my shoulders and sets me on the edge. "I didn't want you to think differently of me."

Sam purses her lips, her annoyance clear. "You're telling me, I've been missing out on all that because you were scared to tell your *best friend* you liked a little frolicking in the woods?"

I roll my eyes, twisting her by the shoulder so I can wash her back. "It wasn't worth the risk at the time. Primal is still so new to many people, and I just... I don't know. Bambi, I wanted to play it safe. Better to have you in my life as a friend than nothing at all."

"I hate you think so little of me. Meanwhile, I've been out here, bored out of my mind, dating boring ass suits when I could have been getting railed in the forest by the man I've loved since I knew what love was."

A deep ache radiates across my sternum. It's a combination of elation and regret; anger that I didn't trust her sooner with this part of me. Threading a hand through my hair, I toss the loofah on the hook. "You're right, and I'll spend every day you let me, making it up to you."

Sam twirls back around. "I owe the same to you. Ever since the day you pushed me in the mud, I always thought that was you rejecting me. Putting me in the friend zone permanently. But now I see, we missed an opportunity, but not our chance. We have that now."

My lips stretch into a wide, involuntary smile. "For a person who's so soft and mushy, it's hard to believe you want someone who's hard and rough around all the edges."

She shrugs, wrapping her arms around my neck and perching on her tiptoes to place a quick kiss on my lips. "What can I say? It also doesn't hurt that you want to take care of me after. It feels pretty damn good."

"Have to keep my prey in good shape. Wouldn't be much fun to chase if not."

Sam laughs, the sweet sound winding around every tight muscle left and melting them into butter. "So you want it to be challenging to catch me?"

Something I can't make out shimmers in her eyes as she rakes a hand down my stomach. My abs tense and flex as she moves over each one. I'm relishing the feeling of finally being touched by her in the way I've craved for so long.

"Yes. It's the hunt and the fight I crave. The need to subdue my prey in order to rightfully earn my prize."

"I see." She nods, a mischievous smirk curling one side of her lips. "Well, in that case, catch me if you can, number twenty-four."

Before I realize what's happening, the glass door swings open, and Sam sprints from the shower. It only takes a second to reach her, but when I wrap my arms around her wet waist, she manages to slip from beneath my grasp.

The beast in my chest roars to life as I grab her again. Our slick bodies fall over the bed, and we begin the best wrestling match we've ever had.

Our limbs tangle as I try to get her hands above her head. She wriggles and flails, her breath coming out in pants as she gives it everything she has to free herself. I drop my head and open my mouth wide, my teeth clamping down on her shoulder.

She yelps, bucking her hips up and pushing her pelvis straight into my erection. I growl, need surging through me as she continues to fight. She really doesn't make it easy, both of us too wet and slick with residual soap to get any type of grip. Every time I manage to secure a hand, she wrangles it free.

It takes far too long, but I finally get a good grip on both of her wrists and shove them above her head, squeezing them tight. I move my knee on top of her clenched thighs and bear down, forcing her legs to part.

She makes me work to lift my knee, but when I press my thigh against her warm entrance, her head falls back, and she grinds against it, creating a friction that makes her eyes roll back.

"Need more already, huh?"

She smiles. "Maybe. Or maybe I just wanted to see if you'd be able to catch me while slippery."

This makes me laugh. "Learned about it two seconds ago and already testing out theories?"

Sam's eyes flash back to me, and I lose myself inside them for a moment. Flecks of black and gold give them a dimension that has always captivated me. Plus, the color reminds me of the bright mud I pushed her in all those years ago. Just another piece of evidence that proves she was made for me.

"We've already wasted so much time, why not jump in?"

I shake my head and huff. It blows her hair back, revealing a speck of green. I pull it from her strands and smile when I realize what it is.

Holding it up in front of her, she mirrors my expression with a broad smirk as she takes it from me. "A four leaf. How appropriate."

I lean down and kiss her nose. It will be the last soft gesture she gets until she's shaking from her next orgasm. "I think so. Sets the precedent for what's to come."

She arches a brow. "That we've been anointed to be blessed with faith, love, hope, and luck?"

The meaning behind the four leaves, an anthem our parents would speak over us when opening the hotel. "Having the luck of the Irish sounds good to me, Bambi."

"Having you inside me sounds better." Her lids flutter as she tosses the clover on the nightstand and opens her legs wider for me.

I oblige, moving to seat myself between her legs and hold her steady. I love the smirk on her face, the one that says she thinks she can handle me. It will be fun to watch her come undone.

And I do. Four lucky times.

Samantha

EPILOGUE

This is unfair. Completely and inexplicably, wrong.

But really, it just doesn't make sense. I've spent *months* learning the city I thought I already knew. I've studied blueprints and maps, and everything else that could help me plan my runs and escape routes.

In the end, none of it does anything to help because the better I get at hiding, the better he gets at finding. Which is good in a sense, because when he catches me, *ugh swoon*, but also, it's incredibly frustrating because it means hunts never last more than fifteen minutes, and I've learned I *love* to run.

Last month, I decided to devise a plan. A full-proof way to outlast the usual time and get him to cry uncle–a word we still haven't needed.

It's summer, and with most people starting their cruises and summer vacations, the hotel is in its slow season. This week, I made sure only the first floor was booked so that the second and third were completely empty.

I was confident that with the split wings, access stairs, and all the rooms, I'd finally get him flustered, so I made a wager.

If he calls uncle, *I* get to hunt *him*. Where if he wins, we do a hunt on the vacation we're taking in the fall. He thinks I'm

shy when it comes to a little voyeurism, but really, this bet is a win-win.

Still, I wanted—*want*—to freaking win.

But the radiating burn in my calf as I make a desperate climb to the roof with Adrian only a few meters behind me, has me on the verge of defeat.

"Come on, Bambi, there's nowhere you can go." The deep rumble of his voice echoes up the hollow stairs. "And if I get you to the roof, I'll fuck you right there for the whole city to see."

A thrill shoots up my spine.

His words sink into my skin, lighting a fuse that reverberates through my limbs. It ignites a new fire for me to keep moving. To keep running despite the ache in my chest and the throb in my clit.

I want to be caught, but I want to win more.

Pushing through the top access doors, I spin around and shove one of the maintenance shovels through the two handles. It won't hold him for more than a few minutes, but that's all I need.

Leading up to today, I placed various things on the roof that I knew would be a good distraction. There're stacks of heavy crates, a few oversized trash bins, and wide industrial laundry carts. All of which are big enough for me to climb through and hide, which will slow him down and allow me to get back inside and run out the remaining six minutes.

I race around and squeeze in between some trash bins on the side of the access doors at the same moment the metal clangs in the air.

My heart bangs into my chest as he slams his body into it again, the sound echoing in the air and making my core clench.

He's hungry today, and it has me reconsidering if I want to continue to run.

Fuck.

No. I need to win. Just this once.

Another few seconds pass until the thick wood shovel splits, clattering to the floor as Adrian slams open the doors. From my position, I can see his back heave up and down with his heavy breaths. His head moves quickly from side to side as he takes in what I've done.

He chuckles. "I will rip this world from its roots to find you before the time runs out, little prey. Now come out."

I bite into my hand to keep the whimper from escaping, the sharp taste of copper tainting my tongue. My nerves vibrate, the need so overpowering it's beginning to wash out the adrenaline.

Still, I manage to suck in a shallow breath and hold it, waiting for the moment he moves enough for me to slip back inside.

A low chuckle falls from his lips as he takes his first step forward. "Have it your way, baby. But when I find you, I'm fucking you until your voice no longer allows you to scream."

He tips a trash can over. "Until your muscles seize from the orgasms."

He smashes a laundry cart over. "Until your pussy is raw and filled to the brink with my cum."

My eyes roll to the back of my head before I squeeze them shut. I'm losing the will. I can feel it slipping with the constant pulse of my clit and the want driving me mad. He's going to win again. He's going to–

"There you are, Bambi." His deep growl forces my eyes to snap open, my heart leaping into my throat as I shriek.

Adrian cages me in on either side of my head before running his nose roughly along the column of my neck. His inhale is deep. "I could smell you."

I watch as the fire rages in his hazel eyes, the need just as strong in him as me. His dark hair is mussed, falling in front of his forehead as sweat drips down his temples. A nerve tics in his jaw as his gaze finds my lips.

"Thirty seconds."

My eyes widen. He's never given me more time. *Ever.* My pulse rages, whooshing through my ears so fast I become slightly dizzy.

"You've already wasted five."

I drop down, dipping under his arm and sprinting back to the door. I don't even make it down a full flight before I hear him call after me.

"Ready or not, here I come."

Adrenaline spikes in my blood, but with my previous plan of escape forgotten, I run for the spare room, my thighs burning and veins throbbing. I nearly catapult inside the room, slamming the door behind me as I attempt to suck in air.

He most likely knew I'd come in here and won't be far behind. I scan the room and make a quick decision to hide under the bed. On quick glance, he may think I'm not here and go check somewhere else.

I only need two more minutes.

Leaping over the bed, I fall to the floor, wincing when I hear the hollow thump of my knee hitting the ground. I know he's probably heard it, but I can't dwell on the mistake and slide under the bed frame.

The heavy pounding of my heart seems almost obscenely loud as it rocks against my rib cage. Pair it with my breathing and I don't stand a chance.

When the door smashes open, I flinch, biting my tongue to keep the squeal stuck in my throat.

The bed skirt is too thick for me to see where he is, but I hear his sharp breaths. He's moving around, unconvinced I'm not in here.

There's only about a minute left. I know it. But before I can claim victory, two strong hands wrap around my ankles and yank me from my hiding place.

I scream out as I kick back, but his hold is an iron grip, bruising my skin as he flips me on my back. Adrian wastes no time ripping my shirt from my skin and tearing my shorts down my legs.

He pauses when he realizes I have nothing underneath, my skin bare, flushed, and ready for him. "Oh, little prey. How fucking perfect you are."

I smile as he peels his own shirt off and frees himself from his joggers. "What time is it, Adrian?"

His nostrils flare when he looks up at the bedside table. I see it when it hits him. When he realizes his decision to give me a second chance caused me to win. His eyes flash down at me, and he smirks. "You win. But for now, I still earned my prize."

Then he slams into me. I screech out, latching my nails into his shoulder blades as I try to adjust to the intrusion. He hisses as he draws out. "*Fuck.*"

He thrusts back in, his pace the hardest it's ever been. I moan as the pain morphs into something delicious, the budding heat already beginning to expand. He leans forward, pressing his flexed abs against my stomach as he threads his fingers through mine.

The new position allows him to drive in deeper, the sensation making the pressure grow.

But then something cold wraps around my finger, sending a shiver down my arm.

I snatch my hand down and examine it, my heart fluttering when I realize what it is. Attached to my ring finger is a massive pear-shaped diamond, with a halo of smaller diamonds around it.

Epilogue

Immediately, my eyes well with tears, the overwhelming feeling of euphoria clogging my throat.

Adrian moves my hands and presses a soft kiss to my lips. "Marry me, Bambi?"

A warm tear streaks down my face. "Oh, my God, Adrian. Yes. So many times, yes."

I wrap my hands around his neck, letting my fingers dive in his hair and pull him closer. Our kiss is greedy, and as hungry as ever, while we devour each other.

It isn't until later, when we're both out of breath, satiated beyond words, that we finally come down. I'm resting in the crook of his arm, tracing idle shapes on his chest, staring at the gorgeous ring reflecting hues of blue on his skin. His free hand strokes my hair, and I almost think I'm purring, I feel so good.

But just when I think there's nothing more perfect than this moment, his whisper proves me wrong.

"Fourth of July, little prey." He shifts and kisses me on the temple. "You can hunt me then."

My heart soars as I climb on top of him, peppering him with sweet kisses and nips of joy. "I freaking love you."

Adrian chuckles, allowing me a few more seconds before flipping me back over. "I love you more, Sam."

The End.

Preview of Liberty Falls

Aria

Men.

I swear that three-letter word is enough to envoke a thousand different emotions from just a handful of women.

For me, the majority of the time, it's annoyance. Whether it's from some type of superiority complex, the lack of common courtesy, or the way that they can never seem to find *that spot* again, even after I just said *not* to move.

Don't get me wrong, I'm not anti-men or anything. But heaven help me, some men—particularly the asshole captain over at the Liberty Falls Fire Station—make me glad I have ol' faithful in my top drawer. Because somehow, even without proof, I *know* he's responsible for my current predicament.

A fire rolls through my gut as I ignore the sharp bite of my nails digging into my palm.

"I'm sorry, Chief Castillo. I'm not sure how this happened."

My heated gaze flashes back to the mayor's timid secretary,

who's doing her best to deliver the bad news. She tucks a blonde strand of hair behind her ear for the seventh time and looks down at the printed Excel document.

She shakes her head in honest confusion before pushing her thin wire frames up her nose and running an index finger across the paper before confirming, yet again, what she's just told me. Her face blooms a dark pink. "It must have been an oversight."

I sigh harshly but internally wince as the girl's face tightens. I know it isn't her fault per se, but the chief in me can't help but hold her to some level of accountability, considering she helps organize the event. "Quite the oversight, Lauren."

"I think it must have been the use of the word 'hot' in his submission. You didn't put that in yours, and that's probably why the system didn't pick it up as a duplicate entry."

I think my groan is inward until Lauren shifts uncomfortably, checking over her shoulder as if looking for help.

"How can a funnel cake be anything other than hot?" I knead my eyelids, trying my best to rein in the obvious agitation in my voice.

I don't mean to be an ass, but my tolerance for mistakes caused by disorganization, or someone relying on technology as if it's infallible, has my patience wearing incredibly thin. In my line of work, those sorts of slipups can cost someone their life.

"Perhaps we shouldn't get so upset at such a small mistake." The deep baritone in the voice behind me sears every nerve I have in unison. I grind my teeth together, preparing for an argument, but my opponent decides to add a little gas to my already smoldering fire. "I'm sure we can figure something out."

Figure something out.

Figure. Something. Out.

For nearly a decade, I've worked my ass off for my current position. Straight out of college, I came back to my sleepy

96

hometown and took a position as a law enforcement officer. I worked under my father for years before he was forced to retire due to double knee replacements, and then the mayor appointed me as the chief of police over the department. It sounds like a huge accomplishment at my age, and while it partially is, in a city with a population of only about twenty thousand people, and a generation of Castillos being in the same position, it wasn't much of a decision on the mayor's part.

Especially since there was no one else who wanted it.

I mean, for one, it's not very exciting. The extent of my job rarely goes beyond making sure the local kids don't get too high and burn down the Jenkins' wheat farm, or helping Mrs. Jackson with the daily cat-in-a-tree catastrophes. The latter is technically a job for the firefighters, but I like Mrs. Jackson. Not to mention it's hard to resist the Irish coffee she makes me while dishing out some town gossip.

Honestly, though, I'm sure it also made it easier for the mayor to have someone that already knows the budget, or lack thereof, which brings me back to the problem at hand.

Because of the small funds allotted, the city throws a Fourth of July carnival every year where local entities such as the police, fire department, as well as the different art departments at the high school host fundraising booths. The funds earned have helped us immensely during the year and without their success, we wouldn't be able to afford some of the "non-critical" upgrades.

Last year, my officers and I had a funnel cake stand that did incredibly well. So amazing, in fact, that when the forms for our booth selections were emailed in May, it was a no-brainer. Since I didn't receive word that there was anyone else who chose the same fundraiser, I went and got all the necessary supplies. Some of my deputies even had their kids paint signs.

Imagine my surprise when the day of the carnival comes

around and I'm blindsided to learn that my booth is next to the fire department's, which just so happens to be selling the same. Fucking. Thing.

So, while I'd love to *figure something out*, I'm afraid that time has come and gone.

On better judgment, I decide to ignore the asshat behind me and force my attention back to Lauren. She's young, only having worked for the mayor a few years, but since she herself was once a participant in the carnival when she was in high school, she knows how important it is not to have active competition.

"How about we look and see who submitted their proposal first?" I ask, knowing it won't matter. It's too late for either of us to switch, but now, it's just to prove a point to the fire captain.

I hold my breath as Lauren's nervous gaze falls back to the paper, and at the same time, a tingle radiates down my spine. A telling sign his stare is locked on my back. I readjust my belt before letting my hand fall to the small pepper spray at my hip. I haven't ever had to use it, aside from that one occasion when a rat with rabies decided I needed to be his next meal, but I may have thrown it at the captain once. Or perhaps twice when he's pissed me off enough.

He grunts in response, his amusement evident, which only irritates me more.

Lauren sees something that makes her turn an even darker shade, but after running a hand through her blonde strands, she's able to steady her voice. "I didn't organize it by time submission when I exported the Excel sheet. So, I only have the date, and both of you filled out the form on May fifth."

"Can it be looked up on the computer?"

She winces. "I deleted the file after everyone filled it out."

"Of course you did." Resignation and annoyance work hand in hand as they force me to finally turn around.

Goddamnit.

Captain Ford stands relaxed a few feet behind me, a smug smirk pulling up one side of his stupidly perfect lips. His black tactical pants and fitted uniform shirt with the fire station insignia leave nothing to the imagination. The fabric is tight across his broad chest, the seams at his arms appearing to be made from magic thread as they stay intact through the constant strain. He lifts a brow, which is naturally arched—another thing I can't stand about men. Can someone explain why they always seem to have perfectly manicured eyebrows, thick lashes, and lush hair from using a two-in-one shampoo?

Like myself, he got his position when he was young, a generational advantage over the nonexistent competition. We were raised only a few houses down from one another, and our parents were constantly visiting each other. Both sides were always big on sharing stories and comparing their jobs, as well as the accomplishments of us kids.

I don't think it was ever in bad taste, but it created a competition between him and me, and soon, everything we did was to spite each other.

If he ran six laps during PE, I had to run seven. If I got a ninety on a math test, he had to get a ninety-one. If I dated the quarterback of the football team, he had to date the head cheerleader. This went on for years, and there was no corner of our lives that the rules of our competition didn't touch. So, when we ended up at the same college, I wasn't surprised.

Luckily, the police academy and the firefighter training program don't occupy the same space, or else it would have been chaos. I can almost picture it now—pranks, ruined clothes, missing shoes.

All of those examples fuel the logic behind me *knowing* that he did this on purpose.

Both our departments get together quite often for drinks

and good conversation. Since our ongoing rivalry isn't a secret, it comes as no surprise that one night, a short time after last year's carnival, I got a little carried away, telling everyone about how the firefighters didn't make half of what my officers did. So, it only makes sense that he would figure out a way to finagle doing the same damn fundraiser.

It takes the full extent of my self-restraint not to say anything and merely walk past him.

Naturally, he doesn't let me get two feet before he ruins my relatively peaceful exit. "If you can't handle the heat of competition, you know you can just stay out—"

"I'd advise you to choose those next few words wisely, Kameron. Because last time I checked, you gave your latest girlfriend food poisoning. So I'd say it's you who needs to stay out of the damn kitchen." I continue on, relishing in his annoyed scoff as I all but stomp away from the assignment table like a toddler having a tantrum.

But as always, he has to have the last word. "Is that right? I mean, it was your mother's recipe, so…"

This forces my feet to a stop, and when I spin on my heels, I'm only half-surprised to see him a mere yard away. A stupid smirk is etched on his face as if it's permanent.

I narrow my eyes. "Bullshit."

He shakes his head, his dirty—no, *muddy*—blond strands falling over his forehead as he lifts two fingers. "Scout's honor."

Something between a strained laugh and scoff tumbles past my lips. His audacity is at an all-time high today, and it's clear he's trying to shake me up. Perhaps this is part of his plan to throw me off and win this game of ours. Too bad I intend to call his bluff.

"My mom would never trust you with—"

"Her trick for making her blueberry scones super thick and buttery is to freeze the—"

100

I nearly tackle Kameron as I slap a hand down shamelessly over his mouth. My own lips are parted in shock as I spear him with a menacing glare, both daring and threatening him to utter another word.

I can feel his smile stretch wider, his lids lowering in premature, victory smugness.

But being this close, with my chest nearly touching his, and the vibrant hues of his irises so clear I can make out three shades of blue, there's something else lingering in them. Something much more dangerous than his usual challenge.

The look makes my breath catch in my throat, and I tell myself it's from the shock of my mother's recipe betrayal that has my heart suddenly hammering into my rib cage. It has *nothing* to do with the heat from his body enveloping mine, despite the already warm air. It's *definitely* not his comforting amber scent or the way his gaze is dragging down my face, as if this is exactly what he intended.

"Asshole." My voice is nothing more than a heady whisper as I yank myself away from him and rub my offending hand on the hip of my shorts.

Kameron's smile stays intact, along with the fire burning brighter in the corner of his eyes. "Perhaps I'll make you a batch sometime, Aria."

I smirk, trying my best to keep an air of being unbothered, because I *am* unbothered. "The day I put anything of yours in my mouth will be the day I swallow fire."

This makes him chuckle. It's throaty and deep and I utterly loathe the way it always makes my stomach do a weird type of flip. Probably because I usually hear it after he wins at something and I want to sock him in the jaw.

"How about a wager, then?"

I lift a brow, my hand finding my hip. "I'm all ears."

He takes a step forward, and though I know I should move

back, I don't allow him to win our standoff and straighten my spine instead. He stands only a foot away now, our chests almost reunited, forcing me to glance up to meet his eyes.

"If the firefighters make more money in tonight's booth, I get to put something of mine in your mouth."

I guffaw at his innuendo, ignoring the way it makes my stomach clench. I tilt my head to the side. "And *when* I win?"

Kameron shrugs. "Whatever your little heart desires."

My favorite part about our bets is when he finds himself being extra cocky and allows for open-ended bets. Nine times out of ten, those are the ones he wins, but when he doesn't, the payoff is all the sweeter.

"What do you say, Firefly?"

He moves just enough to hold a hand between us. I don't hesitate to grab it, and do what I've always done, and shake.

"Deal."

Acknowledgments

Thank you, my reader, for filling your time with the stories in my head.

As always, thank you to my hubs who made this book possible with wrangling the kids and cooking me yummy meals. To my kids for always walking in when I'm writing the spiciest scenes. And to my incredible alphas and betas.

Lo, M.L., Salma, Matti, Alexis, Andrea, Chanel, and Garnet.

Y'all are the effing bomb and I hope you never leave me! Thank you for putting up with me being so last minute and needing everything done in one day. Like seriously. I love y'all.

Extra special thank you to Lo for helping me take on this beast of a trope. (Pun intended)

Thanks to my amazingggggg editor. Mackenzie, girl. Has anyone told you lately you are the best thing since vibrators? Like girl. You're the fucking best and I love you. THANK YOU. For everything.

And Ria, my back and forth and back and forth, I don't know how I got so lucky but you are incredible.

Thank you to Charlton over at https://forbiddenwritings.blog/ tag/primal-play/ for information on primal play.

Again, thank you to everyone! I can't wait for the next holiday I randomly decide to pop one of these bad boys out! Stay tuned.

But I will say, if you're not subscribed to the newsletter, you will be missing out on these two come forth of July.... *winky face.

About the Author

Hey there! My name is Lee. I like to think of myself as a bibliophile who belongs to the Ravenclaw house.

I write romances that can sometimes be sweet and spicy or deadly and kinky. I'm a firm believer in happily ever afters and men who always make sure their woman is satisfied first.

When I'm not writing, I'm drowning myself in a good book, losing track of time on the Nintendo Switch with my kids, and laughing or *yelling* at one of my husband's practical jokes. (He likes to leave fake spiders and roaches around.)

Also, something important to note. I live off Chai and Dean Winchester.

Visit me on Instagram or TikTok to find out about upcoming releases and other fun things! @authorleejacquot